"RAE, ARE YOU FRIGHTENED? . . ."

"Frightened?" she asked, turning around.

One moment the sizzling lightning bathed his tall, athletic frame in light, its strange reflection in his eyes; the next moment, he was clothed in semi-darkness. The air was so still in the room that she parted her lips for breath and gazed up at the darkened figure, the face turned toward her, the man not touching her, yet seeming to. She was not sure if the vibration she was feeling was from the thunder or from somewhere deep inside.

"Maybe I am afraid," she said, her voice a whisper.

"The fear of a storm is a healthy respect," Lucas said. "Even those trees which have weathered many storms and have grown strong and tall and seem indestructible, can be reduced to shreds in a storm like this. No matter how mature or strong, they are quite defenseless against the forces of nature."

"Defenseless," Rae breathed as his face came nearer, suddenly illuminated, and a tremendous rumble of thunder set the hills to quivering. The crash was that of a cymbal.

In response Rae clung to him, trembling, as vulnerable as the time-worn trees. All sorts of things could happen in a storm like this. All sorts of things. And they were happening—in her mind, in her soul, in her heart.

SMOKY MOUNTAIN SUNRISE

Yvonne Lehman

Serenade/Serenata
BOOKS
of the Zondervan Publishing House
Grand Rapids, Michigan

All the characters in this book have no existence outside the imagination of the author. All of the incidents are fiction and pure invention. None of the characters, having the same or different names, bear actual resemblance to persons known to the author.

SMOKY MOUNTAIN SUNRISE
Copyright © 1984 by The Zondervan Corporation
1415 Lake Drive, S.E.
Grand Rapids, MI 49506

ISBN 0-310-46562-1

Edited by Anne Severance
Designed by Kim Koning

Printed in the United States of America

84 85 86 87 88 89 / 10 9 8 7 6 5 4 3 2 1

To Louise
Whose song inspired the theme of this book

MOUNTAIN MAN

Mountain man, a rugged man
Whose frame is lean and leathern
As one who lives with giant hills
His home is nigh to heaven.

Mountain man, a loyal man
He loves with depth and feelin'
In pain and sorrow stands like steel
His faith is strong, revealin'.

Mountain man, a lonely man
Whose gaze is far, revealin'
His words are few, and smile is slow
His wisdom is inspirin'

Mountain man, a learned man
In nature's realm of schoolin'
His refuge is the One above
The God of Spirit rulin'.
  —Louise Barker Barnhill

ACKNOWLEDGMENTS

My deepest gratitude to Janie and George Pickering, owners of Camp Rockmont for Boys, who provided the setting for this book. Camp Rockmont is located in the Blue Ridge Mountains of Western North Carolina, awe-inspiring with its incomparable beauty and panoramic views, and is situated on the site of the former Black Mountain College.

CHAPTER 1

"ANDRÉ'S IN TROUBLE!"

Rae glanced up, startled by Mimi's explosive announcement as the girl rushed into her office and flung herself into the nearest chair.

With another school year behind, Rae had been cleaning out her desk drawers. Now she paused to study the beautiful brunette who gazed at her with soulful blue eyes. One could never be sure when Mimi Doudet was serious or merely exaggerating.

"Why do you say that, Mimi?" she asked, now stacking papers into a cardboard box.

"I don't really know . . . " She hesitated, confirming Rae's suspicion that Mimi didn't mean her brother was in *real* trouble.

"Why don't you tell me about it while you help take those books off the shelves. We're not teacher/student now, you know. Just friends."

"Fine friend you are, making me work on a hot day like this!" Despite the protest, Mimi smiled in her

7

winning way and walked over to the bookshelf, lifting her shoulderlength hair from her neck.

"Hottest May day ever recorded by the weather bureau in Atlanta, Georgia!" Rae reported, mimicking the noon-day weathercaster. "Now, tell me about your brother."

"He's in Florida."

Rae glanced at her. "That's bad?"

"It's *strange*." Mimi forgot the books and leaned back against the shelf. "Both Uncle Lucas and André had planned to stay in Switzerland for another week. When I told Uncle Lucas that you had invited me to spend this week with you, he was delighted. Now," she spread her hands in frustration, "André has called me from Florida and started asking about you."

"Me?" Rae straightened immediately, surprised. She'd never met André, but she knew Mimi was from a wealthy and close-knit family. "Does he make it a habit to check on all your friends?"

Mimi laughed. "André wouldn't check on my friends. But it seems he *does* want to check *you* out!" She shrugged, then the typically mischievous look sparkled in her eyes. "Maybe he's between girls!"

"That's ridiculous, Mimi."

"Not for André," she countered.

"Let's get these things packed." Rae's tone was no-nonsense now. "The sooner it's done, the sooner we can enjoy the air conditioning in the apartment."

With that inviting idea, Mimi returned to her chore with renewed enthusiasm, but she couldn't resist talking about her brother. "At first he asked about you casually; then he got real interested when I told him how terrific you look."

"He wouldn't think so if he saw me today," Rae

8

contradicted, touching her hair that curled into tight ringlets when damp. She could feel the tiny beads of perspiration on her face.

"Anyway, he's coming here," Mimi continued.

"Here? To the university?"

"No, he's going to pick me up at the end of the week at your place. Then we'll drive home to North Carolina together."

"Really, Mimi," Rae said with a sense of exasperation, yet affection for this girl who always twisted things out of proportion. The famous André Doudet was linked with beautiful women from all over the world. He certainly wouldn't be interested in someone he'd never seen. "That explains it. There's no trouble. It's just brotherly love. You don't spend much time together, so this is just a good chance to catch up with you."

Mimi was shaking her head. "He was more interested in you than in me. And André doesn't like to drive. He always flies if possible. Oh, are these the exams we took today?"

"Don't you dare touch those!" Rae warned. "I haven't graded them yet, and when it comes to exams, I'm all teacher, and you're still the student. But you don't have to worry about your grades."

"On the written part I do," Mimi moaned. "Come to think of it, I don't think I could *ever* be as good as you in the gymnastics routines, either"

"The teacher is supposed to excel," Rae chided gently, accepting the compliment.

"I'll bet when you were my age, you were better than I am *now* ," Mimi said with admiration.

"I had the best possible teacher," Rae reminded her and caught her breath. They grew quiet and the

9

only sound was that of books and papers being piled into boxes.

Both women were remembering Rae's teacher, her father, who had died a few months earlier. A famous coach in years past, he had sent several young hopefuls to the Olympics before coming to teach at the university in Atlanta where Rae had been on the faculty for the past three years.

"School's out at last!" Mimi piped suddenly, lifting her arms into the air and dispelling the reflective mood that had momentarily settled upon them.

Rae smiled, remembering the years she had uttered those words as a student, then as a teacher. But it was different this year. An entire summer without her father was not appealing. It would be lonely. Her spirits lifted as she remembered that Mimi would be with her for a week. And that week would be climaxed by a visit from André. It wasn't often one had a chance to meet an accomplished athlete like André Doudet.

"Looks like everything's packed," Rae said after taking a quick look around the office.

As they lugged boxes through the gym, Rae's mind replayed the physical education classes she taught there. Her favorite this year had been *gymnastics moderne*, in which she had had an opportunity to exhibit her extraordinary skills along with her instruction.

After driving the few blocks to the apartment house and unloading the boxes, they collapsed into chairs, enjoying the refreshing effect of the air conditioning.

"As soon as we cool off," Mimi said, wiggling the toes of one foot propped on a box of books, "you and

I are going to have a great week—seeing everything in Atlanta, and doing all there is to do!''

Rae laughed. She didn't doubt that. With her own fair hair and green eyes, she knew that she and Mimi differed in more than physical appearance. In life-styles and temperament, too, they were exact opposites. Mimi was a fun-loving extrovert with the tendency to laugh at life rather than take it seriously. Yet, Rae knew Mimi had depth that rarely surfaced. Rae's faith in God had given her strength to face life with courage after her father's death. But it had been Mimi, herself an orphan, who came offering friendship during a difficult time.

As promised, the week was filled with fun and laughter, then ended all too quickly. Rae had become increasingly excited about André's arrival, for Mimi had proudly pointed him out in numerous sports magazines. ''That's André at Uncle Lucas's ski resort in Switzerland.'' Another pictured the smiling athlete poised on the slopes of a similar resort in North Carolina. He was on the cover of still another, having won the national tennis competition that year.

The only thing that marred Rae's excitement at the prospect of meeting André was the fact that he would take Mimi back to North Carolina, and she would be left to face the reality of her loneliness, and to make a difficult decision about her future.

Rae kept telling herself that Mimi was mistaken about her brother's desire to meet her for any particular reason. After all, they were strangers. Nevertheless, on the day of his arrival, she decided to wear one of her prettier summer dresses. She had tamed her naturally curly hair with hot rollers, brushing it away from her face on one side and

11

allowing it to fall in a soft wave on the other. The long-on-top, short-in-back style was ideal for one so active and complemented the color her father had often referred to as "spun gold."

Expectantly Rae watched from the porch of the modest white frame apartment house. Mimi ran down the front walk to embrace her brother who was exiting from a low-slung bright yellow sports car. Towering over his sister, his brown hair gleamed in the sunlight. He was wearing casual slacks and a shortsleeved shirt, but Rae could visualize him in tennis and ski wear, stepping from the pages of sports magazines she and Mimi had devoured.

Now this perfect specimen of masculinity was walking toward Rae, flashing the dazzling smile that had the power to charm, even from the glossy pages of sports magazines.

Her green eyes met his twinkling brown ones as Mimi introduced them.

"Call me Andy. Most of my American friends do," he invited, extending his hand. "And tell me why a gorgeous girl like you is named Ray?"

Rae laughed, having heard that question hundreds of times before. "It's Rae with an *e* ," she explained.

"I suspected something like that," Andy teased. "You should have told me about her sooner, Mimi. You know blondes with green eyes are my weakness, especially those with freckles sprinkled across an adorable nose."

"How would I know where to find you?" Mimi quipped, her long hair falling below her shoulders as she turned her face toward his. "Last month it was Paris and Switzerland. Then last week it was Florida. Now, you're here!" Mischief played in her eyes.

"What attracted you to Atlanta, André? Was it the red clay, or the Georgia peaches?"

Rae felt that Andy's laughter was a polite recognition of his sister's double entendre, for his glance slid away from her. Sensing his uneasiness, she recalled Mimi's premonition that he was in trouble.

"Shall we go inside?" Rae invited, holding open the screen door.

"I made your favorite drink," Mimi said as she and Andy followed Rae into the kitchen.

"Sounds like lemonade," he said, smiling down at Mimi before pulling out a chair and taking a seat at the small round table. "It's nice of you to ask Mimi to stay with you this week, Rae."

"It was my pleasure," Rae assured him. "Mimi and I have become close friends since my father died."

"Your father was Raymond Martin," Andy said, his eyes lighting with sudden realization. "I didn't make the connection when we were introduced."

Anyone seriously involved in sports knew the name. In addition to his coaching, Raymond Martin had helped to make the gymnastics program at the Atlanta university one of the finest in the nation.

"I'm sorry to hear about it," Andy continued softly. "The sports world has lost a great man. Mimi and I know about that kind of loss. Our parents died when we were both quite young. But there was always Uncle Lucas and Gran. Do you have relatives?"

"No, and I think that makes losses easier to bear. But I try to think not so much of what I've lost, but of what my father has gained. My mother died ten years ago. At least now I have the consolation that they're together again—in heaven."

Rae spurned the grief that threatened to overwhelm her. Feeling Andy's intense gaze, she was grateful when Mimi brought the glasses filled with lemonade.

"Is Uncle Lucas back home?" she asked.

Andy shook his head. "He won't be for a couple of days yet. We'll get home before he does, even by car." He tasted the frosty beverage and nodded appreciatively. "Good lemonade."

"Nothing's too good for my big brother who loves me so much he wants to drive me all the way from Georgia to North Carolina," Mimi replied with exaggerated playfulness, cutting her eyes toward Andy.

"Well, there is another reason, Mimi—something I must discuss with you." He seemed uncertain whether to continue as he poked absently at a lemon slice. "As you know I had to make a trip to Florida. That's where I picked up that little gem out there."

Rae assumed he meant the car.

"Okay, what's her name?" Mimi asked, amusement coloring the inflection of her voice.

Andy's look of chagrin confirmed his sister's assumption that a female was involved. "We have a long drive ahead of us, Mimi. We'll talk about it later." He turned his handsome face and charming smile in Rae's direction. "Right now, I'd much rather talk about your friend here."

Mimi tugged at his shirt sleeve. "You know I have no patience, André! Besides, Rae doesn't mind. We've shared many personal things."

"I couldn't burden her with this one," Andy said, but Rae had the distinct feeling he wanted to talk about it, and her curiosity was aroused.

"It wouldn't be a burden, Andy," she assured him. "If you want to talk about it, I'm a good listener."

14

With a sigh Andy leaned forward, propping his elbows on the table.

"There *is* a girl," he admitted. "Celeste imagines herself in love with me. Her parents wrote to Uncle Lucas, mentioning wedding plans. I was shocked when he confronted me with that news, so I had to go to Florida and see Celeste. I think I've convinced her to make a clean break, but I don't know. . . ."

Mimi shrugged, "Oh, André, you've been in worse situations. What about . . ."

Interrupting, Andy shook his head. "This is different. Uncle Lucas feels I haven't been honest with Celeste. That I haven't made my intentions clear from the beginning. He doesn't like her parents' getting into it, and he even mentioned the possibility of a breach of promise suit."

"Can't you explain to your uncle that you made a mistake, Andy?" Rae asked. "Tell him Celeste misunderstood your intentions?"

"He doesn't take such things lightly, I'm afraid," Andy assured her.

"Sounds like a happily married man who enjoys matchmaking," concluded Rae.

"No, he's a bachelor and vows to stay that way. It's just that he strongly believes in being responsible for one's commitments."

"He doesn't like women?"

The quick note of ironic laughter shared by Mimi and Andy dispelled that notion from Rae's mind.

"He likes women just fine. The problem is," Andy paused, looking sheepish, "that this is not the first time something like this has happened."

"You *have* left a string of broken hearts around the world," Mimi scolded affectionately.

"It hasn't been all one-sided, Mimi," he protested. "But that's the way Uncle Lucas is beginning to see it. He says there have been too many indications that I'm not being honest in my relationships."

"Why doesn't your uncle let the two of you work out your own problems?"

Andy shook his head. "Celeste's parents involved him when they wrote to him, and he feels responsible since he's my guardian. Besides, it hasn't been easy working things out with Celeste. You know how it is when a woman believes she's in love and wants to get married."

Rae lowered her eyes to her glass. No, she didn't know. She had had a few casual dates, a few kisses, but nothing that threatened to disturb her placid existence. In her twenty-five years she had been content to bask in her father's love, and to devote herself to making her parents' last days as joyous and meaningful as possible. Now that they were gone, her world revolved around her work. She now felt happiest, most fulfilled, on the balance beam, the floor mat, and the parallel bars. Here she could be herself—expressing her innermost feelings within the rigid constraints of the sport.

"Celeste wanted to bring her parents to our home to meet Lucas," Andy was saying. "That would be disastrous for a girl like that. She would take one look at the place and believe herself even more deeply in love. You can't imagine what that girl has cost me in clothes and jewelry." He took a deep breath. "Now we have matching cars."

Noting the shocked expressions on the girls' faces, Andy looked from one to the other. "It was *her* idea," he said helplessly.

"André, didn't you tell her you were through with her?" Mimi almost shrieked. Rae, though silent, found the idea equally incredible.

"Yes, but Celeste is not the kind of girl one drops suddenly. You've heard the proverb about a woman's wrath? No, this will have to be done carefully and discreetly."

"Well, if Uncle Lucas plans to invite them to the house, what hope is there?" Mimi's voice sounded despairing. "He'll insist you marry her."

Andy traced a pattern on the tabletop. "I lied to Uncle Lucas."

"Oh, André," Mimi moaned. She reached over to take his hand and his fingers tightened around hers. His expression was more that of a remorseful little boy than a grown man of twenty-six. "What did you tell him, André?"

"The only thing that would make any difference. I told him I had been wrong about Celeste and was going to Florida to make her understand. Then I said I couldn't marry Celeste because," Andy paused, cleared his throat, then continued in a desolate tone, "because I had fallen in love with the perfect girl, the kind he always wanted for me. A nice, Christian girl!"

Mimi looked delighted. "Oh, André, have you?"

"No," he admitted, shaking his head. "I haven't exactly been looking for that kind of girl, I'm afraid."

The three sat in silence, staring at cold lemon slices resting on ice. Rae knew only that Mimi's older brother had graduated from a university in Switzerland and helped to manage his uncle's ski resort there when he wasn't playing in tennis tournaments all over the world. He had probably earned his playboy reputation, she thought.

She could well understand how females would be attracted to André. Physically and materially, he had much to offer. But from this brief encounter, she suspected he lacked the spiritual qualities that would make a long-term relationship possible. He needed guidance, but seemed instead to be manipulated by what she supposed was a domineering uncle.

Mimi's concerned voice broke through the wall of silence. "Did Uncle Lucas believe you when you told him you had fallen in love with a Christian girl, André?"

Had it not been such a serious matter, Rae would have laughed at the scowl on Andy's face as he imitated his uncle in a booming voice, " 'Fantastic, Andy! She must really be some girl if you're thinking of settling down. Go to Florida. Clear up this misunderstanding with that young woman and her parents. Then bring your perfect girl home. I want to meet her. Within the week! Otherwise, I'll have to take drastic measures which includes cutting your allowance' "

"You see," Andy explained to Rae, "I don't come into my inheritance until I'm twenty-eight." He looked helplessly at the two women. "Then he told me if I didn't bring my fiancée to North Carolina, he was going to do what he should have done in the first place and invite Celeste and her parents to our home." Andy grimaced. "If he finds out I lied on top of everything else, I'm doomed! My only chance is to come up with a girl Uncle Lucas would approve—a nice, Christian girl."

"Oh, André," Mimi sighed in exasperation, but love for her brother glowed in her eyes. "How do you manage to get mixed up in such scrapes?"

Their laughter was tinged with irony. Mimi had already confided to Rae some of the childish pranks she and Andy had instigated while growing up. And Rae was well aware of Mimi's impulsive nature, which included extravagant shopping sprees. Remembering her years at the university, Rae suspected, too, that the lively girl had left her share of broken hearts behind.

The laughter subsided as they sat trying to think of a solution. Rae traced a design through the moisture collecting on her glass, while the silence grew increasingly uncomfortable. When she looked up, Andy and Mimi were staring at her with a peculiar gleam in their eyes. Almost simultaneously, they broke into triumphant grins.

Rae swallowed hard. A strange sensation crept over her. *Heavens, what must they be thinking?*

"More lemonade?" she asked in a strained voice. They shook their heads. Rae rose from the table, gathered the glasses and took them to the sink. Looking out the window at the backyard, she noticed the brilliance of the sunshine bathing the new growth of the leafy trees. Twin maples. After his first heart attack, her father had spent much time under the shade of those trees.

Rae returned to the table, aware that Mimi and Andy were watching her every move. Under their scrutiny, her fair complexion was fast becoming a scarlet flush. Finally she sank into the chair, shaking her head.

"Rae." The confidence in Andy's voice indicated he had found the answer to his dilemma. In spite of the physical differences between brother and sister, there was definitely a family resemblance. Now it was one of sinister determination.

"Oh, no!" she cried in dismay, their incredible scheme suddenly transparent.

"Oh, come on, Rae! You could do it. You could pretend to be André's fiancee. And we wouldn't have to pretend about your being a Christian." She turned to address Andy, "Rae and her father headed up the Christian Athletes Club on campus."

"I'm impressed," he said. "As Uncle Lucas would be." He leaned across the table and took Rae's hands in his. His voice was low and persuasive. "Would it be so unthinkable to be engaged to me for a short while, Rae?"

"Andy, it wouldn't work." She was adamant. "Just tell your uncle how you feel."

"You don't know my uncle!" he replied, as if such an admission were out of the question.

Rae could agree with that statement. She *didn't* know Lucas. Mimi had made frequent references to him in their late-night talks. She knew that he acted as guardian and provider to his wards, but he had remained a distant parent figure in Rae's mind. One she found rather foreboding, now that she thought of it.

"I'm sorry, Andy," she said. "I wish I could help. I really do. But it just isn't possible."

"Well," André sighed. "At least I *thought* I had found the solution. *Do* you have plans for the summer, Rae?" he asked, apparently dismissing his scheme.

Rae withdrew her hands from Andy's. Studying one pale pink-tipped nail, she thought about his question. She had not signed the contract to return to her position at the university in the fall. The administration and faculty had been more than understanding and sympathetic throughout her father's illness and death, assuring her that the position would remain open indefinitely. Now, she felt, a complete change was in order. But she hadn't yet decided what that would be.

Rae looked around the kitchen of the cozy apartment. She and her father had moved here over two years ago when they sold the house. They had been fortunate to find a rental so near the campus. Now that she was entirely on her own she had wondered if she should renew her lease at the end of the month or go away for an extended vacation to think about her future.

"I'm not sure, Andy," she admitted finally. "I've considered a vacation. I may even try to find a summer job. A change of scenery might be good for me."

"A job?" Andy's eyes lit up. "I have the perfect job. And for a teacher of gymnastics, who is also the daughter of Raymond Martin, it would probably *seem like a* vacation. Our summer camp for young athletes opens up in June."

"André, how ideal!" Mimi said, her eyes bright. "You should see Rae when she's teaching. She's *magnifique!* Everyone loves her, but she commands respect, too. And she makes us believe in ourselves— that we can do anything we set out to do. She could head up the gymnastics program. She's equally good in swimming and. . . ."

"Wait a minute," Rae protested. "You don't know if your uncle would approve of me as an employee,

21

even for the summer. The job sounds challenging, but I just don't know . . ."

"I understand," Andy said finally, a look of resignation settling on his face. "There's a special guy here. There would be for a girl as attractive as you."

Rae recognized his ploy, tried to keep the blush from her face, but knew she was unsuccessful. "No, there's no one special."

A strange silence followed. Then, without taking his eyes from Rae's face, Andy addressed Mimi. "You know, Mimi, I believe Rae is the kind of girl Lucas has in mind for me. He thinks my friends are too flashy, too worldly, too caught up in materialism. Rae is sensible, sweet, and probably the most honest person I've ever met—not to mention the most beautiful."

"Flattery will get you nowhere," Rae said quietly, quite afraid she was in error. She wished she had thought of something more original than an old cliché.

"I'm not trying to flatter you, Rae; I'm even beginning to understand your viewpoint. We aren't exactly infidels, Mimi and I, although we probably appear that way to you. I can see that it would be against your principles to pretend an engagement." He leaned forward. "Tell you what—I won't ask you to do that. Just come with us to North Carolina and consider taking that summer job. Be my special girl for the next few weeks. Perhaps you don't find that idea too unpleasant."

"It's not unpleasant at all, Andy," she assured him. "I'd love the job, but . . ."

"But you can't accept the offer?"

"Oh, Andy, not under the circumstances."

"Don't you like me a little, Rae?"

"I barely know you."

"Don't be difficult, Rae," Mimi pled.

Rae knew there was no way these two impetuous siblings could understand her reluctance. But sensible people just don't do things like that.

"All right," Andy said with resignation. "I won't ask you to pretend anything. Just let me tell Uncle Lucas that you're my girl, from my point of view. Is it so unthinkable that I could take you seriously? And is it so impossible that you might consider really being my girl?"

"Well, no," Rae admitted, "as long as I don't have to pretend a relationship that isn't there." She gasped to realize how close she was to agreeing to Andy's scheme. Being André Doudet's special girl did have its appeal, even to a sensible girl like her. She quickly reminded herself that Andy wasn't really taking her seriously, but needed a girl in a hurry to get him out of a jam. If she remembered that, she could guard against ending the summer with a broken heart.

A change of scenery would be good for her, and could provide the opportunity for the serious thinking she had to do. She was well aware that her funds were not unlimited and she must soon decide what direction her life should take.

Yet, there seemed to be so many reasons why she shouldn't accept this offer. *Mimi will be in Paris during the summer*. Rae remembered.

"I would be a stranger there."

Andy shrugged. "There will be plenty of people around. Our summers are very busy. And I promise you won't be lonely."

"Your uncle must be"—she stifled the urge to say, "an old tyrant," and substituted—"very strict."

"As I mentioned, without Uncle Lucas, there's no allowance," Andy explained. "He holds the purse strings."

"And the purse," Mimi added, laughing.

Andy grinned. "True. Until we're married or twenty-eight—whichever comes first. And for me, twenty-eight is a few years away yet."

"But, Andy," Rae persisted, "I might not meet your uncle's requirements. I'm really a very ordinary, uninteresting person."

Andy looked amused. "And you are well-trained in gymnastics—an excellent reason why he would hire you!" Then he leaned closer. "But if he doesn't give us his blessing, I'll marry you anyway!"

"Oh, Andy," she laughed helplessly. At least the summer promised to be anything but dull.

CHAPTER 2

THE LOW, SLEEK SPORTS CAR sped around the mountainsides like a small yellow bird, flitting from treetop to treetop before eventually nestling in the heart of the Blue Ridge Mountains.

Around every bend of the Parkway was another scenic delight—deep, emerald valleys; rocky ravines slashed with crystal waterfalls; tangled thickets of flowering shrubs carpeting the forest floor on either side of the highway. The retreating sun flung visual blockades as subdued peaks of blue and green were thrust against a graying sky. Wide-open landscapes, endless highways, and skyscrapers had given way to a world of almost primeval splendor, and Rae wished the sun would linger so she could drink in the beauty of this paradise.

"It's incredibly beautiful," she whispered reverently.

Andy reached across the front seat of the car and squeezed her hand. "This part of the country compares favorably with any spot in the world," he said. "At times I take it for granted, but you have a way of making me appreciate things, Rae. As if seeing them for the first time." Giving Rae's hand a final squeeze, Andy turned his attention to the serpentine curve ahead.

Rae had not felt comfortable with his one-handed driving, yet felt sure her apprehension was due to her own lack of familiarity with the mountains, for he maneuvered the car expertly, even in the fast-approaching darkness of night.

Turning her face toward the window, Rae concentrated on the fascinating world opening up before her. The closer they came to their destination, the more intrigued she became. There was a sweet fragrance she could not identify, and the pungent odor of pine.

Soon Andy turned off the main road onto a paved private one. The car began its curving ascent as it wound higher through trees that joined limbs in a conspiracy against the moonlight.

"It's like a jungle," Rae said in wonder.

"The only place in the world where there is a greater variety of trees is in China," Andy informed her. "Around this next curve, you will find our haven from this crazy, chaotic world."

After the turn, both sides of the road were flanked by rustic, split-rail fences. Orange trumpets on long green throats swayed and bent, heralding their coming. Suddenly, like a mirage, the great stone structure appeared. Mellow light gleamed from windows, and floodlights illuminated the landscape. Rather than dominating, the two-story structure blended majestically with its surroundings. Circular wings did not distract, but conformed to the natural undulations of

26

the land. Behind the mansion rose an even higher peak, darkened by the night, as if it were some strange sleeping beauty.

Rae could not begin to comprehend what the scenery must look like in bright sunlight, for even now, shadowed by darkness and lightly bathed with artificial light, the colorful array of springtime was much in evidence. Even her brief glimpse provided the spectacular picture of the fragile among the stately, the delicate in the midst of strength. There were dark evergreens; leafy maples; yellow-green poplars; pink and white dogwood blossoms; and bushes laden with purple, red, pink, yellow, and white flowers.

At the beginning of a long sweeping drive was a rustic wooden sign with the words *Mountain Haven* carved into it.

"That's Lucas's name for the house," Andy explained.

It was a place like none Rae had ever seen. The stone mansion with its great expanse of glass windows seemed to draw nature into itself, and at the same time the shingled roof appeared to touch the sky.

Andy didn't turn onto the drive bordered by natural rock and lush greenery, which circled in front of the house, but drove onto a secondary gravel drive, around a stone wing, then came to a stop beneath a redwood roof.

As soon as they stepped from the car, Rae was bombarded with a sweet fragrance. "Strawberries!" she exclaimed, inhaling deeply.

Mimi laughed and pointed to a row of bushes along the stone wall. "That's calycanthus," she explained, "more commonly called 'Carolina allspice'."

Rae walked over to them. The blossoms looked like rust-colored wooden flowers. When she touched them, they felt like wood, but when she sniffed, they smelled nothing like wood.

Each taking bags, they climbed the redwood steps alongside the stone wall leading to a high deck at the back of the house.

"It must be something in the air," Rae said incredulously. "Tell me flowers don't look like wood, and rocks don't shine."

"Wrong, wrong," Mimi corrected. "There is mica in the rock, and when the light strikes just right, it *does* shine. These stones were hewn out of our own area mountains."

Rae stood on the deck for a moment, marveling at the sounds of nature, almost deafening in the absence of car horns, train whistles, and airplane engines.

Andy took their luggage upstairs while Rae and Mimi whipped up a quick snack which they ate at the kitchen table. After the snack, Mimi checked the lounge for mail, leaving Rae and Andy to tidy up.

As they worked, Rae thought of the past two days and Andy's helpfulness with arrangements she had had to make before leaving Atlanta. Their close proximity during the drive had provided an insight into his personality. His interesting conversation had been flavored with humor and intelligence as he related experiences associated with his many travels. She was growing to *like* this roguish charmer.

Her parents' illnesses had occupied her time and thoughts during recent years, so Rae had not seriously considered a life's mate. But in the back of her mind was the assumption that the man of her dreams would be both a Christian and an athlete. Andy certainly fulfilled one of those requirements. And the other was partly her responsibility in this world: to set an example for unbelievers. Yes, with a faith in God to put his priorities in the right order, Andy could become the kind of man a Christian girl could consider seriously.

Their fingers touched as they reached for the same dish. Andy grabbed her hand and lifted it to his lips just as Mimi came in from the lounge, carrying a bundle of letters.

She held an envelope toward the light. "Wonder what Isobel has to say," she mused.

"Better not snoop in Uncle Lucas's mail, Mimi," Andy reprimanded her, and Rae wondered if his irritation was caused by Mimi's interruption or by the letter.

"Who's Isobel?" she asked curiously.

"Very likely the future mistress of this house—if she has her way," Andy explained. "She's a widow with a young son who very much needs a father. So she has set her cap for my uncle."

"You really think they'll marry?" Mimi asked. She didn't appear happy about that.

Andy sighed, as if resigned to the situation. "They've been seeing each other for quite a while now. Wouldn't be surprised."

Mimi nodded in acquiescence, shuffled through the letters, gave Andy his mail, then returned to the lounge with the other letters.

"We should say good night, Rae. Tomorrow's a big day."

She knew he was referring to the fact that tomorrow she was to meet his Uncle Lucas.

His face grew pensive. "It's not going to be so bad, is it, Rae?"

Although she hadn't yet absorbed her new surroundings, Rae was looking forward to working in a mountain setting. And she believed Andy needed her as a buffer against his uncle. But there was something else to consider.

"Much depends on what your uncle thinks of me, Andy," she reminded him.

His hand touched her shoulder and he spoke reassuringly. "He'll like you, Rae. Any man would. But the important thing is that he believes I want to marry you."

Rae sighed. "The burden's on you then, Andy. I'm only supposed to be thinking over our relationship."

His smile was warm. "I don't think it's going to be at all difficult." He leaned close to whisper. "I suspect we've already convinced my sister."

Rae turned her head in time to see Mimi step quickly back inside the lounge doorway. She looked up curiously at Andy but he only grinned and said, "Good night, Rae. And thanks for everything."

Mimi rejoined Rae only after Andy had gone upstairs and closed the door to his bedroom. Approaching Rae, she shook her head. "André surprised me tonight," she said. "He's treating you like someone very special."

Rae laughed it away. "Mimi, you're imagining things. Your brother's just being polite and charming. It seems to be part of his nature."

"It is. But I know André. He doesn't seem to be acting." She stopped on the stairs, her lovely eyes aglow. "You and André! Rae, that would please me so much."

"Don't be silly, Mimi. Andy isn't looking for a girl like me."

"And why not?" Mimi asked.

"Different backgrounds. He's rich, I'm poor. He's internationally known, I'm relatively unknown. He's . . ."

Interrupting, Mimi stopped on the stairs, her hands on her hips. "That sounds like you think we're terrible snobs. And I sincerely hope you aren't calling me a snob, because if you are, I'll challenge you to a duel of–of racquetball."

"You know you always beat me in racquetball."

"That's why I chose it!" Mimi laughed, and they walked up the stairs arm in arm.

In spite of her exhaustion, Rae couldn't sleep.

The cool mountain air, moist and misty, drifted in through the open bedroom window, stirring the curtains. Outside, the shadowy hulk of the mountains spoke of permanence and endurance. She was glad she had come. But there was something mysterious and compelling out there in the night that beckoned to her on air heavily scented with the perfume of a thousand unknown blossoms.

Tossing the coverlet aside, she rose and put on her robe, tying the sash around her tiny waist. The flimsy garment was designed for comfort on hot city nights, she realized too late. Glimpsing her reflection in the mirror, she shrugged. *No one will see me*, she reassured herself.

Quietly she closed the bedroom door. Her slippers made no sound on the carpet in the upstairs hallway. Following the light from a lamp that had been left on, Rae made her way down the stairs, looking up momentarily at the exposed beams of the cathedral ceilings.

This is no mountain cabin, she thought. She reveled in the aesthetic blend of log and hardwood and beam that carried the hallmark of a sensitive designer, just as the out-of-doors bore its Creator's mark.

Leaving the back door ajar, Rae stepped out into the night. She crossed the redwood deck, walked down the steps to the second deck and on out to a third that was completely surrounded by a veritable jungle.

Inhaling deeply, she savored the wonderful, musty fragrance of earth and trees and wild, growing things. Somewhere a gurgling stream made its noisy way down the mountainside. Insects sounded a symphony, and night birds called to their mates. Everything here was so wild, so untamed, so free, and she responded with a sense of exhilaration she had never felt before.

Lifting her face to the cooling breeze, her eyes were met by the sight of lush foliage—the intertwining branches of the trees so dense that only slivers of moonlight penetrated to splash on her face and hair, turning it to gold.

She wasn't sure how long she stood there, listening to the night music, absorbing the peace, before she heard his footsteps. They were heavy, swift, hesitating only momentarily to locate her. She did not turn to look. It would be Andy. He wouldn't be able to sleep, either.

Her eyes were closed when his arms slid around her waist, and she did not open them when he turned her toward him, but lifted her face willingly. His lips met hers with a thoroughness that surprised her.

She had expected, would have welcomed, a sweet,

gentle kiss. But the intensity of this encounter shook her. Feeling his strong hands gripping her arms, Rae gasped and pushed herself away.

"You're not . . . Andy!" she whispered.

"No," he said in a bemused voice, still holding her in a tight embrace, his eyes slowly sweeping her face, the wide, frightened eyes, the soft, parted lips. "And you're not Isobel."

Rae shook her head, unable to look away.

"You a friend of Andy's?" he asked, his eyes lingering on her face.

Rae nodded. There was no mistaking who *he* was. And he was nothing like she had imagined. There was no way she could ever call this man "uncle."

"You must think me impulsive—kissing you like that," he murmured, a smile tilting the corners of his mouth.

The man reminded Rae of the unknown that had so intrigued her about the night—fascinating, wild, and untamed. His shirt sleeves were rolled up and the neck of his dress shirt was open, as if he had recently discarded a tie.

"Yes," she said finally, "I–I thought you were Andy." It occurred to her that not only was she surrounded by beauty in this place, but there were things out there in the night to be wary of—like bears and snakes and who knew what else?

"Forgive me," he breathed. "I didn't mean to frighten you." And he released her, somewhat reluctantly it seemed.

Still, his very nearness was disturbing. Something about him was like the unknown wilderness beyond the safety of the railing—compelling, deep and mysterious, captivating. And something deep within her stirred, reaching upward toward the light and warmth, like some fragile forest flower. She was aware that she was part of something greater—and that things could never be quite the same again.

Sensing her discomfort, he moved away, putting a respectable distance between them.

"What is your name?" he asked.

"Ramona," she whispered, looking up into his eyes, amazed to discover that the sensation was the same as when she had first glimpsed the mountains. There was majesty here, power, and unspoken challenge. "I-I mean Rae," she corrected herself, using the familiar nickname with which she had been tagged ever since the day she had begun toddling after her father, imitating everything he did.

The man's voice was soft, melodious, flowing over her wounded spirit like a spring rain. "Ramona," he echoed her given name.

The sound of it restored her to reality. No one ever used that name—except her father.

The man reached out to wipe away the tear that trickled down her cheek. "And now I've made you cry? Why?"

Rae didn't know how to tell him that she didn't understand her own behavior, didn't know why her emotions were suddenly as unpredictable and precarious as the mountain roads. Perhaps it was his gesture that had moved her so. It was such a gentle touching—like the soft sweet caress of the night mist.

Turning from him, Rae stepped into the shadows. "It's just that no one ever called me Ramona but my father . . . and he died recently."

"Do you mind if *I* call you Ramona?" he asked kindly.

"No," she shook her head, and found that she didn't. Rather than feeling a stab of loss, it brought a flood of warm memory and she turned her face toward him again with a faint smile. He did not smile back but gazed at her in a strange way that she could not fathom.

"Have—have we met before?" she asked, some vague impression forming in the back of her mind.

"That's not a very original line," he said in an abrupt change of mood, taking a step nearer. "Now," he said, reaching out his finger to trace a pattern down her nose and around her soft, parted lips that trembled beneath his touch. "Wherever did Andy find you? Tell me what acting school you're from, or how much Andy paid you for this little job and I'll repay him. Then you and I can get on with more pleasurable things."

The insinuation in Lucas's tone began to penetrate Rae's consciousness. Was he intimating she was like some of the women in Andy's past? But what else could he think? She had even admitted she thought he was Andy—as if she were there on the deck waiting for him.

Suddenly aware of her attire, she grasped her robe closed in front, then turned and fled across the decks as if some wild beast were in pursuit.

Breathless, she slammed the door of her bedroom harder than she intended, and, without turning on the light, went to the window that overlooked the area she had just left. The dark figure stepped into the light and looked up, as if knowing where she would be. She moved out of sight and sank on the edge of the bed, taking in great gulps of air. How could she ever face the man again and behave normally? Or more to the point, would she ever *be* normal again?

After taking off her robe in the darkness, Rae climbed beneath the covers that Mimi had insisted would be needed. "The nights are quite cool here," she had said.

Rae shivered in spite of the down coverlet. She could not dismiss the tangled emotions she had felt with that mountain of a man. No one had ever evoked such a response in her. In those brief moments he had touched something deep within her that she hadn't known existed. Then he had casually dismissed the moment with his accusations. But what could he think of a girl who not only allowed him to kiss her, but responded to it like that? After all, they were strangers. He was the *loathsome* Uncle Lucas, who in an instant could cut off Andy's allowance, force his marriage to Celeste, and send her packing!

She tried to rationalize. Perhaps it was because of the loss of her father that she had responded to a man's arms around her. Maybe it was the need to feel cherished and safe. *No,* she whispered into the darkness. It was not her father's touch she needed.

She faced the window, looking out past the billowing curtains, breathing in the misty cool air. The stars were huge, almost as if she could reach out and touch them. Everything here seemed larger than life.

Tossing restlessly, she knew sleep would not come. Hers had been troubled nights since her father had become ill many months ago. She had simply accustomed herself to dreamlike snatches of sleep. There would be none at all tonight, it seemed, but perhaps she could will her body to relax. *Inhale. Hold for a count of ten. Slowly release the breath, allowing tension to drain away. Inhale . . .* It was a technique she had used before gymnastic competition. It always worked. Tonight it wasn't working at all.

She thought of Andy. He resembled his Uncle Lucas. Maybe that's why Lucas had seemed so familiar. Even Andy's voice held a quality that might someday mellow into the same resonant tones as his uncle's voice. But Andy's eyes were not as dark, nor was his hair, nor was his skin. Andy wasn't as tall, nor his shoulders as broad, nor his body as muscular, nor his grip as firm.

"Oh, no," Rae breathed, as if in prayer. "I know what it is now. Andy is like a shadow compared to his uncle." She liked Andy. In fact, she more than liked Andy. His masculinity, his charm, his good looks, his youthful vulnerability appealed to her, and she had even looked forward to getting better acquainted.

Now she knew that Andy, in comparison with Lucas, was but a reasonable facsimile. Andy was a hill that could be conquered; but this man was a mountain too steep to scale. He was rocks and cliffs and sheer drop-offs and ledges.

Exhausted, Rae lay with her eyes closed, and, though she did not sleep, she did not open them again until the early morning hours.

Rae was instantly aware of a difference in the atmosphere. Getting up, she pushed the curtains aside. She had expected to see a spectacular view of mountains and trees and valleys beyond. But she could see nothing through the dense fog.

Opening a suitcase, she pulled out a pair of shorts and a long-sleeved shirt and dressed hurriedly. Brushing through her hair, she left the room, retracing her steps of the early morning.

The patter of her tennis shoes stopped abruptly when she neared the back door. He was there, with his back turned to her. The mist seemed to be swirling about him, threatening to invade the house. He had changed into jeans and a plaid shirt.

"Don't you ever sleep?" he asked, without turning around. She wondered how he knew it was she. But Andy would have spoken. And Mimi would have called a cheery greeting and rushed forward to embrace him.

Rae took a deep breath before answering. "I have slept very little since my father died several months ago."

"You'll find this place to be very conducive to rest." He paused, as if wondering how long she planned to be a house guest. "Are there relatives?"

"No. No one. Oh, friends, of course . . ."

"Like Andy."

"And Mimi," she added.

He turned toward her and in the early light of day his face astonished her. It was as handsome, rugged, commanding, frightening as she had remembered, and she caught her breath.

His eyes swept over her trim, perfect figure. She was accustomed to admiring glances. But this appraisal seemed different, as if evaluating, perhaps deciding if she were a suitable friend for his niece and nephew. And after their first meeting, how could he think so?

He took a step forward and Rae abruptly moved back.

"You're afraid of me," he said incredulously. "Aren't you? Did I cause that? Or have you been told

38

that I'm some kind of ogre? Or, is this some kind of act?''

''I'm not an actress,'' she answered truthfully.

''If you belong to Andy, I shall give you no reason whatsoever to be fearful of me. If Andy is serious about you, then I will not attempt to interfere with that. That's how it is.''

His words held the ring of truth and Rae felt a terrible longing that nothing could be done about. This morning she had experienced the first real kiss of her life, and he seemed to be saying, ''Forget it, it won't happen again.''

Before she could speak, he was asking if she would like coffee.

''I was going to run,'' she said.

''Again?'' he teased and a grin played about his lips.

She knew he was making a joke about her having run from him on the deck during the early morning. But she could not help but respond with a smile, seeing a strange warm glow in his eyes. It crossed her mind that it might be wise to run from him now. He reached for her hand and she did not move away.

''You'll need a guide,'' he said, leading her out onto the deck where they became enveloped by a velvet fog. Soon they fell into step on a pathway. ''The fog is a precarious thing. It may have obscured the entire mountain range for miles, yet we can walk through it for ten feet and find the sun shining through.''

Rae's eyes brightened at the prospect. ''I've never experienced anything like the feeling the mountains give me,'' she said. ''And I've seen so little of them. I can hardly wait to see more.''

Just at that moment Rae stepped on a twig and

tripped. Instantly Lucas's strong arm was encircling her waist, preventing her from stumbling and falling. With his arm around her, she felt completely safe, and she proceeded with confidence.

Maybe it was her lack of sleep, Rae surmised, or maybe it was the mist that rendered the world so dreamlike, so lovely, so different from anything she had ever seen before. The scene was like a lady dressed in all her finery, with the fragrance of perfume to complete the effect.

Just as Lucas had promised, there were spots on the climb where the fog had dissipated, and rays of golden sun peeked through leafy branches. A light breeze stirred tender young leaves. Moisture lay heavy on the pink blossoms of rhododendron, azaleas, and mountain laurel.

Stopping at a stream, they scooped up handfuls of cold, clear liquid and drank laughingly, wiping the drops from their mouths. Then Rae followed him to higher ground until, finally, he stopped on a rocky ledge. The fog lay below them, obscuring whatever lay in the valley that stretched on forever before rising to another peak, and yet another.

"Does it never end?" she asked in wonder.

Lucas laughed lightly, enjoying her discovery. "It's different each time you see it. Here," he said, reaching for her hand, "front-row seats."

She climbed down onto the ledge which provided not only a seat but a back on which to lean.

The sun was turning her hair to gold, making a halo of the dampness that had transformed the soft wave to little tendrils of natural curl.

"I'm accustomed to vigorous exercise and running every morning," Rae defended her heavy breathing, "but I haven't been in top shape since . . . for several months. And this is different." She gestured toward the valley. "The air here seems thinner, cleaner. It takes my breath away."

As if knowing instinctively what she was thinking, he said quietly. "You've had no one to comfort you since your mother died."

Rae bit her lip and frowned thoughtfully. "My father and I were a great comfort to each other. My mother was so brave during her illness. Even then she reached out to others, and her Christian faith inspired me to reach out in my health. It's true that some good comes from even the worst situations, if we keep believing in God."

Rae looked up then, to find Lucas staring at her in a different way—sort of a studied, interested way—and she felt he would understand if she continued.

"I know mother is in a better world," Rae said distantly, looking out into the distance as if seeing that other world. "But," she admitted, "it's still hard to go on without those you love. My father was never the same without her. I think his missing her eventually led to his stroke. I was not enough for him."

"We need God in our lives," Lucas agreed. "But we also need people with whom we can share the hard times." He lifted her chin with his forefinger and forced her to look at him.

"I thought he was enough," she replied in a thin voice. "He's the only man I ever really cared about."

Rae did not immediately understand the expression in his eyes as they searched her face. "The only man?" he finally asked with skepticism. "What about Andy?"

What about Andy? Her mind was clouded and she

41

had to look away from his questioning gaze. Turning her head, she saw the fog hovering over the unseen valley. Though she couldn't see it, she knew the valley was there, just as she knew that somewhere beneath this strange upheaval, this indefinable convolution of Lucas, was Andy. The vague impression began to register that her reason for being here was Andy.

How much could she say without betraying Andy's confidence? Without endangering their tentative friendship? Her relationship with Mimi? Summer job possibilities? She would try to be as honest as she could possibly be.

"I haven't known Andy very long," she said truthfully. "But I hope to know him better before the summer is over. He offered me a summer job, so I'll be working with him—" she quickly added, "that is, if you agree."

Lucas's silence and thoughtful expression puzzled her. Perhaps he would question her job qualifications. Instead, his words were tinged with incredulity.

"Andy told me he had met a Christian girl who was special to him. . . . I didn't believe him."

Rae didn't know what to say. To be completely honest with Lucas would mean she must damage her budding friendship with Andy. She suddenly felt caught in the middle of something and she had the strange feeling her relationship with Andy was not going to be quite so simple as remaining silent while he pretended she was his special girl. But that was something she would have to work out with Andy.

Sighing shakily, Rae leaned her head back against the rock. She was aware of extreme fatigue accompanied by a quivery feeling, something akin to the sensation of having practiced for too many hours on the athletic equipment.

"What will happen to the fog?" she asked.

His dark eyes now seemed to hold a strange resignation as he looked away from her toward the valley below. Rae closed her eyes, listening as he talked in the deep, resonant tones that both excited and soothed her. He was as much a part of the mountain as the rock on which they sat.

"Sometimes it drifts away," he was explaining. "At other times, it clings to the mountainsides. This morning it is rising. Soon it will envelop us. Then it will become thinner, and the sun will shine brightly as if the fog had never existed."

Turning her face toward him, Rae breathed in the odor of his clean, fresh, vital masculinity and knew a man like that would never wear a sweet-smelling fragrance. The out-of-doors was fragrance enough.

"What are you thinking, Ramona?"

The sound of her name, as her father had spoken it, touched her deeply. And she found herself pouring out her heartache over the loss of her parents, her indecision, her loneliness. Her voice droned on and on while Lucas sat beside her, silent, immovable. At the moment he did not seem to be a stranger at all, but someone in whom she could confide, someone for whom she had been waiting, unaware, all her life.

She spoke of her mother and father who had both coached gymnastics at the famous school, of the young athletes they had championed to Olympic wins. Ramona had been born when her mother was in her early forties—the child they thought they could never have. Then her mother had become ill and died when Rae was fifteen—the year she was to have won at the

43

Olympic Games. After that, Rae had lost her will to try for the gold. She had gone on to win some national awards, was part of the college team, and had stayed on to teach at the university.

Then, several months ago, her father's stroke had left him physically unable to return to his duties on campus. The doctor's bills from her mother's illness, combined with the new expenses, had piled up. The money was gone, and her own future, uncertain.

Rae sensed, rather than saw, the fog when it lifted to surround them. Her eyes were closed, but she felt the dampness as it enveloped them, then moved away to be replaced by gentle fingers of sunlight.

It happened inside her, too, as the emotion of her losses overwhelmed her, spilled over, then moved away with the mist.

"I doubt that I'll return to the university," Rae said, her voice catching in her throat. "Without my father . . . " She couldn't tell if her face was damp from her tears or from the phantom fog.

"I understand," Lucas said at last, breaking his long silence. "Andy, Mimi, and I faced such a crisis when our parents—all four of them—died in a plane crash in the Swiss Alps. It was such a freak thing. They were young—too young. Acceptance didn't come easily. It had not seemed a real possibility when we talked about my becoming Mimi's and Andy's legal guardian in the event of a disaster. In fact, we joked about it, since I'm only ten years older than Andy. Then suddenly, it was only too real. Mimi and Andy came to me so lost and forlorn, their world in pieces. Their father—a spirited, dashing French-man—was gone. Their mother, my sister—a lovely, exciting woman—taken from them."

44

Rae watched his face, thinking he was so young to have borne such a responsibility.

Lucas smiled at her and sighed deeply. "I may have overindulged Mimi and Andy at times," he admitted, "but I've done my best. And I'm fortunate to have my grandmother nearby with her wisdom and faith. It was through her I learned that dependence on God you speak of." His next words were spoken almost reverently, as though he were afraid he might shatter the spell between them. "I didn't really believe Andy when he told me about you, Ramona. He was right. You're exactly the kind of woman I've always wanted . . . " he paused, adding, "for Andy. Strange as it may seem, he's like a son to me."

His words were no real comfort to her, she realized miserably. She should be glad that Lucas approved of her . . . for Andy.

Following Lucas's lead, Rae braced her feet against the huge boulder in front of them. In spite of herself, she felt herself drifting off into an exhausted sleep.

When she awoke, they were resting in the shadow of the rock, and the sun was blazing high in the sky. Rae raised her head to find Lucas's head thrown back against the rock, leaning to one side, his lips parted in easy breathing. Her shoulder was pressed against his.

As Rae shifted her position, Lucas opened his eyes. Only a second of incomprehension dulled them before he smiled a lazy smile. The stubble of beard was more pronounced.

"Feel better?"

She could only nod. She did not only feel better—she felt newborn, alive!

Lucas stood and stretched languidly. Rae's pulse beat faster at the sight of his supple grace.

"Want to run back?"

"Lead the way!" she answered, eager.

He started slowly, then increased the speed until his long legs were beating the downhill path at a steady, rhythmic tempo. Rae's movements were perfectly synchronized with his. She was so close behind him that when he swept an occasional branch out of the way she was already past it before it could sweep back. Though the temperature had risen with the sun, the trees shaded them as they jogged down the twisting path.

When Lucas's pace slowed, Rae knew they must be nearing the house.

They ran up the steps of the lower deck with Lucas still in the lead. He stopped suddenly, causing Rae to collide with him. Reaching out to break her fall, he encircled her waist, lifted her off her feet for a second or two, then set her down again.

"How was that?" he asked, breathing hard from the strenuous workout.

"Invigorating!" Rae inhaled deeply, then automatically swung her arm around his waist, seeing nothing but his smiling face turned toward her.

They were almost upon the lounging figures on the second deck before they realized there was anyone else in the world.

CHAPTER 3

"I SEE YOU'VE met Uncle Lucas," said Mimi, mischief dancing in her dark eyes. Then she rushed into her uncle's waiting arms, delighting in his hug. Lucas kissed Mimi's cheek and turned to greet Andy.

"I *thought* you might be out running, Rae," Andy said uncertainly. Looking at Lucas, he added, "I didn't know you were back."

Rae thought she must have imagined the tense moment between the two, for Andy stepped forward and Lucas's arm went around his shoulders in an affectionate gesture.

"Let's go in," Lucas said. "We're famished. Mind eating in the kitchen?" he asked, but didn't wait for an answer. Going inside, he shouted, "Selma, where are you?"

When the plump, mature woman appeared, Lucas gave her a big hug. "Now there's a woman for you. Best cook in the world!"

"You know that sweet-talking means nothing to

me," Selma said, but the look on her face denied the words.

Lucas laughed and took a seat at the wooden table. He and Andy sat opposite each other with Rae beside Andy.

"Eggs and ham, Selma," Lucas said.

"I'll get the juice," Mimi offered and went to the refrigerator.

Lucas filled the water glasses from the pitcher on the table. Rae, looking over the rim of her glass, thought of the gurgling stream on the mountainside.

"You look awful, Rae," observed Mimi as she served the orange juice.

Rae laughed. "I don't care," she replied, and she didn't. "I haven't felt so free . . ." she searched for words and shrugged, "*ever*."

"When did you two meet?" Mimi cast an inquisitive eye in her friend's direction.

Rae hesitated, but Lucas replied immediately, grinning. "I would say about two o'clock this morning."

Mimi gasped, and Andy was noticeably paler. "You've been on the mountain all night!"

"Oh, no," her uncle answered. "We took an early morning hike."

"Coffee, anyone?" Andy's voice was distinctly cool. He poured a cup for Rae. "Sorry," he apologized as some of the coffee spilled over in her saucer.

"It's okay." Rae hoped her expression would convince him he had no cause for concern. But Andy had walked back to the breakfast bar to refill the coffeepot.

"When are you leaving for Paris, Mimi?" Lucas asked.

"Next week," she said, her eyes lighting up when she looked at her uncle. Their mutual affection was obvious. "Rae and I are going to have one great week before I go and before she settles down to work."

When Selma appeared, bearing steaming platters of ham and eggs, hot biscuits, and grits, Lucas asked God's blessing on the food.

"You haven't told me your last name," Lucas said, looking at Rae. When she opened her mouth to reply, he continued, "But I know. Your father would be the famous Raymond Martin. He is one reason I sent Mimi to the university in Atlanta. Not only did I want her to have the finest academic training available, but the finest physical training."

The flush of pleasure staining Rae's cheeks betrayed her delight. For a moment it seemed they were the only two people in the room. But she soon became aware of Mimi's wide-eyed stare, and she felt her face grow hotter still under Andy's questioning glance.

Looking at Lucas, Rae saw that a strange grin quirked his lips. "Ramona Martin," he boomed, "we haven't been properly introduced. Welcome to the world of Lucas Grant."

Rae's laughter halted in midair, and her fork dropped to her plate in a clatter.

"*Lucas Grant*?" she gasped. She had only heard him referred to as "Uncle Lucas" and assumed he was a Doudet, too. "I knew you looked familiar, but I thought it was because Andy looks so much like you. . . . You're the Lucas Grant who won the gold medal in skiing, and was expected to win again the year I was fifteen. But you broke your leg on the slopes in Switzerland."

She did not add that, because of the rash of articles

and pictures reporting the event, she had also experienced a painful teen-age crush

Lucas was grinning now. He picked up his fork. "One and the same," he said.

"Why didn't you tell me?"

"It didn't occur to me."

"I cried for you," she said. "That was the year I didn't get to go. Thinking you must feel as disappointed as I, I identified with you."

"Well, thanks for that." The grin was still on his face. "I must have sensed your concern, because the disappointment was not the heartbreak for me that it was for you. I had already proved what I could do on the slopes. And—I had my 'children'." He looked fondly from Mimi to Andy. Mimi beamed, but Andy did not raise his eyes from his plate. "Besides, I was all of twenty-five and you were only fifteen—much too young for me then," he quipped.

"*Then*, Uncle Lucas?" Andy's voice chilled the atmosphere, and the group grew strangely silent. Putting her fork down, Rae leaned back. Had she not known better, she could have easily believed Andy's look of hurt and frustration.

"A figure of speech, Andy." Lucas spoke without malice.

Andy's next words were uttered quietly, but with perfect clarity. "Are you trying to steal my girl, Uncle Lucas?"

Rae gasped and stared from one to the other. "Please!" she whispered but was completely ignored.

Mimi shrugged, apparently not understanding the tension arcing between her uncle and her brother.

Andy lowered his eyes while Lucas studied him thoughtfully. "You know better than that, Andy."

50

"Stop, this instant!" Rae demanded. "You can't talk about me as if I were not here!"

Lucas glared at her. "Please be quiet, Ramona. This is probably one of the most important issues Andy and I have ever discussed."

It was shock that silenced her.

"I don't think you could accurately accuse me of ever stealing a girl from you, Andy," Lucas said, returning his attention to his nephew.

"Not exactly," Andy admitted, "but several of them have seemed to prefer you."

"Oh, this one girl fell so hard for Uncle Lucas," Mimi began, trying to ease the tension of the moment, "that she climbed the high diving board down at the lake in her evening clothes and threatened to jump in and drown if Lucas didn't come 'save' her!"

Apparently unconcerned, Lucas drank the last of his coffee, then held out the cup for Selma to refill. He and Andy did not seem to be hearing Mimi, but were lost in their own private battle.

"Uncle Lucas told her to jump and be done with it!" Mimi continued. "Of course, she didn't, and her audience left, so she climbed down and someone drove her home."

Neither Lucas nor Andy responded, and Rae and Mimi grinned at each other. For a moment it was like the days at school when Mimi had regaled her with wild accounts of childhood pranks.

"This one's special to you, Andy?" Lucas continued to probe.

"You ordered me to bring her here within the week, Uncle Lucas. I know you wanted to get to know her, but . . ." Andy shrugged uncomfortably.

For the first time Andy seemed to have struck a

sensitive note with his uncle. Lucas appeared discomfited, running his hand through his unruly dark curls and stroking the stubble of beard.

"Andy," he began, his tone slightly defensive, "how am I to know which ones you're serious about and which ones you're trying to set me up with? Now, you have to admit you and Mimi have been guilty of that kind of thing before."

"You can tell she's different, uncle," Andy said matter-of-factly.

"Surely you didn't expect me to take your word for that, Andy. As your provider and guardian, don't I have an obligation to make sure you're making the right choices?"

"I think you forget that I'm no longer a child, Uncle Lucas. There are some things I must decide for myself."

"André." Lucas spoke his name with the kind of authority that forced eye contact. "I want the truth. Is this girl special to you?"

Rae held her breath, fearing what was to come. It was apparent that Andy loved and respected his uncle. She was sure he would have to tell the truth. Rae was only grateful that the question was not directed to her.

Andy did not take his eyes from her when he spoke quietly. "Uncle Lucas, Rae is different from any girl I've ever known. And, yes, she is very special."

Rae swallowed hard. She could scarcely believe the ease with which Andy had lied to his uncle.

Lucas cleared his throat. "Well, Andy," he said uncomfortably. "I'm sorry if I was out of line. Perhaps I should have tried to get to know Ramona in your presence instead of alone. . . . '' he faltered, then turned to Rae, ''Did I offend you?''

''No,'' she answered truthfully, shaking her head. ''Oh, no, not at all!'' For a moment she couldn't look away. It was as if her favorite song had been interrupted by a shrill siren to be followed by a recording: *This is a test, only a test. In case of an actual emergency, you would have been instructed to . . .*

So Lucas had been testing her, trying to discover if she was really Andy's girl. The conversation, the comfort and protection of his strong arms had meant nothing. It was only a test.

Lucas turned from her confusion with a mocking smile and lifted his eyebrows. ''What I can't understand, Andy, is how you could have allowed her to be missing all morning without tracking her down. I don't understand you. She has beauty, passion, intelligence, sensitivity. . . . How could you let her get away?''

Rae knew Lucas was trying to laugh it all away. He wanted truth from Andy, yet Lucas himself had deliberately played with her emotions, deceiving her into thinking that he cared how she felt about things. That was despicable! She could not, would not, sit docilely and be discussed as if she were an inanimate object.

''Stop it!'' she protested, rising to her feet. ''Andy knows how to treat me, Lucas. Like a . . . like a . . . lady.'' Her green eyes sparkled defiantly as she lifted her chin.

Lucas threw back his head and laughed heartily. ''That's exactly my point. I couldn't have stated it better.''

Rae's audible gasp was an automatic recoil from the stinging slur. Was Lucas inferring she was not a lady?

"Oh, how could you?" her voice quivered. "How could you?"

Uncontrollable fury gripped her, and, before she knew what was happening, her hands had closed around the water glass and she had dumped it over Lucas's head.

He jumped from the chair so quickly that it crashed to the floor. Rae turned to run from the room, but his hand shot out and grasped her wrist. His expression was fierce.

"I'm so sorry," she breathed, her voice choked. "I don't know what possessed me. . . ."

Water dripped from his curls and ran in rivulets down his face.

"I was not insulting you," he said. "I was referring to the fact that, if Andy wants to keep you, he should start treating you more like the woman you are. He should have been the one to hear about your family, your fears, your dreams." He paused in an effort to control his emotions. "But maybe you need some time to cool off a little, too. After you've rested, you'll feel better."

It sounded like a dismissal, and Rae ran from the kitchen, Mimi right behind her.

In the bedroom, she fell across the bed, thoroughly humiliated. She did not understand Lucas Grant. Nor herself, for that matter.

"Oh, Mimi," she wailed, her voice muffled in the bedspread, "how awful! What have I done?"

"Awful?" Mimi asked, flopping down on the bed beside her. "I don't think it's awful at all. I think it's wonderfully romantic. Don't you see? Uncle Lucas and André are fighting over you.''

Rae sat up, staring incredulously. ''Are you out of your mind, Mimi? It's horrible. And . . . embarrassing. I talked to Lucas about such personal things. Now I've behaved like a—a child. I can't face either of them again. I'm leaving!''

Mimi slung her dark hair behind her shoulders. ''You can't leave now, Rae. André needs you at the camp, and you did agree to help him out.'' Then Mimi's eyes sparkled. ''Where did you find the nerve to pour water on Uncle Lucas, Rae? Nobody's ever done such a thing before?''

''Oh, Mimi! I don't know! I didn't mean to. He'll never forgive me. Now I've ruined everything—for everyone.''

''Oh, no, you haven't. You've just made it more interesting. Really, Rae, it does seem that André was truly concerned—about you, I mean. After all, he did ask you to come here. And it's no secret how attractive Uncle Lucas is to women . . .''

''Oh, hush, Mimi!'' Rae burst out. Suddenly a hot bath and bed sounded very appealing. ''I have better sense than to consider becoming involved in anything like that. If I hadn't, that little scene downstairs just now would have convinced me.''

''Well, there's one thing for certain, Rae.''

''What's that?'' Rae stepped out of her shorts.

''Uncle Lucas obviously likes you. And he has one weakness . . .''

''Lucas—with a weakness?'' Rae jested, her hands on her hips. ''What could that possibly be?''

''André and me!'' she gloated. ''He loves us very

much. He's a strict disciplinarian and has done a marvelous job with us, as you know."

They laughed together, relieving the tension of the past few moments.

"But he has spoiled us, too." Mimi continued. Since André is obviously interested in you, Uncle Lucas will do everything in his power to nurture that interest."

A sudden, inexplicable surge of anger flared again. "And I'm to have absolutely nothing to say about any of this?"

Shaking her head, Mimi replied. "Not a word. Around here, darling, Lucas has the last word. And if André wants you—and I believe he does—Uncle Lucas will get you for him. One way or the other." She walked to the door, put her hand on the knob, and paused as if debating whether to say what was on her mind. "I can't think of anyone I'd like more for a sister-in-law!" she mused and slipped out the door before Rae could think of a suitable retort.

Delighting in the warm shower, she noted how much softer the water was here than in the city. *Fewer chemicals,* she surmised, remembering a crystal-clear stream she had seen that morning on the mountain.

The light spray cleansed her hair and tear-stained face. She determined to put aside any ideas about Lucas Grant, just as surely as she was now washing away the feel of his lips on hers, the strength of his muscular arms around her.

Determined to shut out the disturbing thoughts, Rae shut off the shower, dried herself, slipped into a nightie and slid between the sheets, admiring the feminine room. The decor was antique white and sky blue, with plush blue carpeting matching the patterned wallpaper. Obviously no expense had been spared in furnishing the room, with its solid cherry canopy bed and ornately carved highboy. To one side was an inviting chaise lounge, deep in pillows, and an assortment of interesting reading material on a round skirted table nearby.

She turned toward the windows, where the white curtains seemed always to be stirring from some invisible breeze. Rae must remember her original intent in coming here, before the romance and intrigue of this exotic setting overpowered her. She had come to escape heartache, not to invite more. With a sigh she burrowed her head in the soft pillow.

The next thing Rae knew Mimi was shaking her shoulders and calling her name.

"Rae! Wake up! Come on now. You're sure making up for all those months you couldn't sleep. You've slept all day!"

It took awhile for the words to register. When Rae sat up in bed and looked out the window, she saw the dwindling light of late afternoon.

"It's five-thirty," Mimi informed her. "Dinner is at seven. Hurry! You've only an hour to make yourself beautiful."

Pushing the sheet aside, Rae stretched and yawned. "I've slept like a log. Must be the mountain air. But. . . ." her grin was mischievous as she looked in the mirror at the wilted figure and head full of drab ringlets, "it will take more than an hour, I'm afraid."

"I've plugged in your hot rollers. I'm wearing my red. Wear your green. We'll wow 'em!" Mimi teased, then left Rae to her privacy.

Less than an hour later, with the hot rollers to relax

the tight curls, and a vigorous brushing to bring out the highlights, her golden hair was anything but the tangled mess of the earlier morning.

She never completely concealed the sprinkling of freckles across her small, straight nose for she had been told they were quite alluring. The green dress brought out the color of her eyes and they were shaded by long, dark lashes. She reached for her glossy lipstick to apply to her full, soft lips. A faint blush heightened the color of her cheeks.

Standing and viewing herself critically in the mirror, she wondered what Lucas would think of her now that she looked more like a mature woman who was a teacher at a university rather than an early-morning jogger who cried on his shoulder, or a moonlight temptress who invited his kiss.

She sat down again, losing her nerve. That speculation and pep talk did no good. Her dumping water on Lucas Grant reigned uppermost in her mind, and she was sure he wasn't about to forget that! Facing him again would not be easy.

"What's keeping you, Rae?" Mimi asked, knocking on the door and interrupting her friend's reverie. "Don't you know that you don't keep Uncle Lucas waiting?"

CHAPTER 4

MIMI'S EYES WIDENED when Rae opened the door. "You'll dazzle 'em tonight!"

Surveying the dark-haired girl in scarlet, she shook her head. "Not a chance with you around, Mimi."

Mimi had been one of the most popular girls on campus, not only because of her startling good looks, but because of her effervescent personality. It was in Rae alone, however, that she had confided the deeper longings of her heart.

"Well," Mimi was saying, "I will admit I may have a job keeping Brent at a distance."

"Brent?"

"Oh, I've never mentioned him before, but he would make the 'perfect husband', or so Uncle Lucas insists." She wrinkled her nose. "I can't think about anyone except Pierre anymore—you know that, even if Uncle Lucas doesn't!"

Rae nodded, understanding.

"Pierre!" Mimi exclaimed, hugging her arms to

herself. "I'll see him next week, Rae! Not a word to anyone, though. If Uncle Lucas knew, he wouldn't let me go to Paris. But I feel about Pierre . . . oh, how can I describe it? I know," she said, with sudden insight, "I feel like you looked this morning. You were a mess—no make-up, hair in all those funny little ringlets—yet when you and Uncle Lucas came out of the woods, you were —radiant."

Rae shrugged it off. "Well, we had run down the mountain and . . . oh, come on! We're late."

"I'm glad you're here, Rae," Mimi said sincerely.

Rae wondered how wise it was, her being here. But what else could she do . . . now?

Rae descended the staircase, determined to make the best of the evening. At the landing Mimi went to greet Brent, who was talking with Andy. Rae knew immediately what Mimi had meant about the tall, young man with the handsome face, good clothes, nice smile, and charming manners. When he looked at Mimi, a spark ignited in his eyes. He couldn't conceal his enchantment with the girl in red.

"Now for the blond bombshell," said Mimi under her breath after she had introduced Rae to Brent.

Standing behind one of the two plush couches facing each other in front of a massive fireplace were Lucas and Isobel.

Before the introduction could be made, the woman stepped forward. "You would be one of Mimi's little friends." Rae cringed inwardly.

Upon closer scrutiny Rae realized the blonde with pale blue eyes was not as large or imposing as she had thought at first glance. It was just that so much of her was showing in the shimmering white sheath. No doubt those were real diamonds around her neck and

60

at her ear lobes. Her light tan set off a flawless complexion, as did her dazzling white teeth when she spread her lips into a smile. There was no denying she was sophisticated and beautiful—at least Lucas's age, if not older. So this voluptuous woman was an example of Lucas's preference in women.

Rae suddenly felt angry—angry with herself for caring what Lucas liked or thought, angry with the woman before her whose eyes did not reflect the warmth of her smile. She seemed to thaw a little, however, when Lucas stepped forward and said, "Ramona is André's friend, too. Ramona—Isobel Patrick."

"Well, Ramona. I'm very glad to meet you." Even the voice was well-modulated.

"Rae," she corrected. "Everyone calls me Rae, Mrs. Patrick."

"Oh, you make me feel ancient, calling me Mrs. Patrick. Please call me Isobel."

Rae suddenly realized that Lucas couldn't have possibly mistaken her for Isobel in the early morning. Her gaze swung sharply toward Lucas and found his eyes on her, an amused expression there. Her glance raked his face, taking in the smooth-shaven skin, deeply tanned, the eyes that had seemed so tender earlier. His broad frame was now attired in an obviously expensive formal brown suit with velvet lapels and a beige silk shirt and tie—so different from the mountain man in jeans and plaid shirt of the early morning. This man was cool, self-possessed, so in control of his surroundings, the king of the mountain—a perfect escort for the perfect Isobel.

Suddenly Andy was at her side, offering a glass of ginger ale.

Gratefully, Rae turned to him, surprised at the affectionate look in his eyes. "You're especially beautiful this evening, Rae," he said softly.

Her smile was one of genuine pleasure. "After this morning, I suppose anything would be an improvement."

"Come on," Andy said, "I want to show you something."

They walked around the great stone fireplace that separated the lounge area from the library in which they now stood.

Andy gestured toward the three walls, lined from floor to ceiling with books. "I'm not sure I ever want to read again," he grumbled. "I haven't yet recovered from my college days."

She laughed with him. "I know exactly what you mean. Such torture is not easily forgotten."

He steered her over to a trophy case displaying Lucas's gold medal. Flanking it were other lesser awards, conferred for his superb skiing skills. Some of the trophies were tributes to Andy's expertise in skiing, tennis, and swimming. Listening to Andy now and watching him describe the various meets, Rae realized why women were so attracted to him. He was irresistible when he was talking animatedly about the sports he loved, his eyes alight with his intense passion for the game.

"I've got to talk to you, Rae," Andy said fervently.

"Fine," she agreed.

"I mean—alone. Perhaps we'll have a chance after dinner."

He placed his arm lightly around her shoulders and they walked back into the lounge to find Mimi and Brent.

When dinner was announced, Rae was pleased to see that she had been right in her earlier supposition that the dining room overlooked the decks. Small-paned windows covered almost all the wall facing the back of the house. There were no curtains. None were needed. The effect was that of a rustic setting, as if the jungle outside were an integral part of the room.

"I must see this," Rae said to Andy, then walked over to the windows.

Shadows were stealing across the wooden deck as the sun swiftly made its descent behind the mountains. How different the scene appeared each time she looked at it—once in the moonlight; another time in the mist; again in the sunlight; now in shadows that gave the deep green leaves the appearance of ebony.

"Perhaps she's just one of those spoiled brats who refuse to eat anything as ordinary as paella Valenciana!"

Mimi's banter finally reached her ears, as did the good-natured laughter of the others.

"Oh, I'm so sorry," Rae apologized, quickly taking the seat that Andy was gallantly holding for her. "It's just that it's all so fascinating—so very different from Atlanta. I'm afraid I got carried away."

"The only thing that disturbs me," Andy was saying as he settled himself beside her, "is that Selma might get tired of waiting, take it all away, and serve us grits instead."

To Rae's extreme discomfort, she realized that she had been seated to Lucas's right and that Isobel was on his left, directly across the table from her. She suffered a momentary pang before remembering that she was the newcomer, the honoree at this affair.

Brent and Isobel had obviously dined here many times before.

While the salad was being served, Rae took the opportunity to look about her and was once again reminded of the unique blending of elegance and luxury on the interior with the lush, untamed vegetation beyond. The walls themelves were of dark paneling, like the kitchen. The rectangular room was designed with a brick fireplace at the far end, and Rae could see that two overstuffed armchairs could be drawn up to the fire for conversation or quiet contemplation on a winter evening. She would be gone before winter.

They were seated at a long dining table in gold velvet padded chairs with very high, straight backs, enhancing the aura of formality and precision in this room. Suspended over the table were two magnificent crystal chandeliers and, beneath them, the *pièce de resistance*, bringing life to the otherwise austere surroundings—two huge silver bowls displaying miniature clusters of pink blossoms set against the background of thick, waxy, dark green leaves. They had been gathered, no doubt, from the grounds.

Rae realized she was smiling when Lucas asked, "I'm sure you recall our brief lesson in mountain flora and fauna from this morning?"

He *had* pointed out several plants and identified them during the early morning hours.

"Mountain laurel," she replied confidently.

"Rhododendron," he corrected playfully.

"Oh, yes. Rho . . . do . . . den . . . whatever," she finished feebly.

"Don't worry," Andy consoled her. "It takes time to become a mountaineer."

"Oh, darling—" Isobel touched Lucas's forearm, apparently bored with the conversation—"before I forget, Kevin made me promise to thank you for the card and the lovely game you sent him."

Lucas smiled warmly. "I'm glad he's feeling better."

"Oh, he is. Much. He wouldn't miss opening day at camp for anything!"

André leaned toward Rae. "You are about to discover that Selma is a real *cuisiniere*."

"I'm already convinced," she replied, discovering the hidden delights of Selma's Paella—chicken, vegetables, rice tinted a dull yellow by the addition of saffron. And were those clams? And shrimp! This was more than a meal. It was an adventure.

During dinner conversation, Rae learned that Isobel's home was in Raleigh, the state capitol, and that she and her son Kevin, despite a virus that had hung on for several weeks, were visiting Isobel's parents who lived in nearby Asheville.

The conversation turned to Andy's activities of the past year, then to Mimi's present interests, which led quite naturally to discussion of Rae's summer employment. This bit of information surprised Isobel.

"Will you be staying here at the house, then, after Mimi leaves for Paris?" Isobel asked her.

Lucas spoke before Rae could answer. "She will stay in one of the cottages at the camp—with the other staffers."

"Oh, I see," Isobel said and smiled sweetly. Rae looked past Brent to Mimi, who was making a valiant effort not to laugh. She would have to remember not to glance at Mimi too often. No doubt Isobel would be wondering how Andy had become acquainted with an

65

ordinary working girl. The woman's next question proved her correct.

"I'm always interested in romances," Isobel said brightly. "How and when and wherever did you two meet?"

Andy answered immediately, "On one of my stops to see Mimi in Atlanta."

"Oh? Love at first sight?"

Rae felt a stab of resentment at Isobel's assumption and her patronizing tone.

"Something like that," Andy replied and returned to his eating, as if the discussion were closed. But where Isobel left off her questioning, Lucas took it up.

"I would have thought a sensible, intelligent girl like Ramona would not believe in love at first sight. Perhaps you are speaking for yourself only." His tone sounded accusatory and Rae suspected he had not totally accepted Andy's apparent sincerity.

"I don't think love is necessarily *sensible*," Rae said defensively, looking directly at Lucas, "or reasonable. It can be quite disconcerting, unpredictable, and unexpected." She had at least *read* about that kind of love. "I think the important thing is whether it is treated lightly, as some passing fancy, or treasured for a lifetime."

Lifting her chin, she determined to meet Lucas's sarcasm head-on, but discovered something surprising in his eyes. He looked as if he could not agree more.

Blessedly, Mimi started up a conversation about Brent. Now twenty-two, he would receive a master's degree in business in another year, then would go to work in his father's firm.

"Where he will eventually work his way up to the

presidency," Mimi informed Rae. "It will probably take all of five years."

"Well, I think dad plans to hold that position for a while yet," Brent countered. "But it is a real possibility for the future." The way he looked at Mimi indicated he would be happy to have the beautiful girl as a part of that future.

Rae knew it was not Brent who interested Mimi. Her heart belonged to Pierre. Mimi's thoughts were with him, too, for she began to speak of Paris, fashions, and trips abroad. Isobel, quite a traveler herself, joined the discussion enthusiastically.

Invariably the conversation drifted back to sports— a subject Rae never tired of.

"Ramona's father was a famous coach," Lucas informed Isobel and Brent.

"Rae," Isobel corrected, and smiled condescendingly.

"I'm allowed to call her Ramona," Lucas replied.

Rae picked up her spoon. She didn't dare look at Lucas but busied herself with the dessert.

"Her father called her Ramona," Lucas continued in his explanation. "I represent an uncle figure, I suppose."

"That's certainly refreshing," Isobel said, laughing lightly. "How many more of those diving board episodes could one stand?"

Disliking the implication, Rae could not resist a retort. "You needn't worry. I could tumble off a diving board, do tricks in the air, or dive in with my mouth wide open, and still not drown."

Lucas laughed heartily while Isobel's smile still did not reach her eyes.

"A fish, huh?" asked Lucas, still laughing.

"At least half," she replied, glancing at Mimi who winked.

"And I know what the other half is,"Lucas said, as all eyes turned to regard him curiously.

Rae drew in her breath and held it for a long moment.

"A gymnast!"

Mimi immediately began telling of Rae's athletic abilities, including her medals and honors.

"I suppose I would be classified as just a home-body," Isobel said.

"If telling your maid and housekeeper what to do classifies you as a homebody, I suppose you're right," Lucas said, chuckling.

"Now, Lucas," Isobel reprimanded, placing a well-manicured hand on his sleeve, "I'm turning into a regular gourmet cook. And I can prove it. I insist on cooking for you one evening soon."

"I suppose I'll have to take you up on that," he responded.

After dinner Isobel regretfully announced that she had to return to her young son. Taking her arm, Lucas led her from the lounge to show her the gifts he had brought back from Switzerland.

Unsuccessfully stifling a yawn, Mimi stretched luxuriously. "Guess I'm still tired from the long drive from Atlanta."

Taking the hint, Brent stood to leave. "Some of the gang are coming to my place for a luau on Friday. Would the three of you care to drop in—especially since it will be Mimi's last night in the States for a while?"

"We'd love to!" Mimi replied, then rose. "I'll walk you to the car."

As soon as the couple had left, Andy moved closer to Rae. Emotionally drained, she had leaned her head back against the couch and closed her eyes. At the touch of his hand on hers, she opened her eyes.

"Rae, it's time for that serious talk," he said.

And then Mimi and Lucas were back, lounging on the sofa opposite them, and Andy released her hand and reluctantly moved away.

Lucas removed his tie, then unbuttoned his shirt at the neck as if, now, for the first time since dinner, he could truly relax.

"You managed to get rid of Brent in a hurry," he scolded Mimi fondly.

"Like you managed to get rid of Isobel?" she asked with a saucy toss of her head.

"It's not the same and you know it."

"To tell the truth, Uncle Lucas," she pouted, "I could hardly tear myself away from him."

Lucas snorted. "You could barely tolerate him, you mean!"

"You know me pretty well, huh?"

"For several years now," he said, nodding.

"But you've ruined me for all men, Uncle Lucas. Not one of them can measure up to you."

"None?" he asked quizzically.

"Almost none," she replied, stealing a glance at Rae. They exchanged knowing smiles.

"Anyway," Mimi said, looking back at Lucas, "I promised Brent he could come by and take me to church in the morning."

"Be back in time for lunch, Mimi," Lucas said. "Gran is coming to meet Rae. Would you like to worship with Gran in the morning, Andy?" he asked his nephew.

"Sure," he replied, "if Rae wants to. It really doesn't matter much to me."

Rae's voice was quiet, but firm. "It matters to me, Andy."

The soft music from the stereo did not fill the uncomfortable silence that followed.

Ever diplomatic, Mimi hurriedly changed the subject. "Is extra help coming in next week, Uncle Lucas?" she asked.

"Marie will be here on Monday morning." His voice held a note of wry humor. "Don't worry. You won't have to do your own laundry."

"I did plenty of it at school. But that reminds me," she said, jumping up, "I'd better see what I have to wear in the morning."

As soon as Mimi left, Andy excused himself, too. "I'll be right back," he said to Rae. As he walked through the doorway, he was removing his tie.

"How long have you been here?" Lucas asked when they were alone.

"Almost twenty-four hours," she said and looked down at her hands folded stiffly on her green dress.

His next words echoed her thoughts. "Incredible!" he said under his breath. "It seems much longer. I feel I know all there is to know about you."

CHAPTER 5

"YOU HAVEN'T EVEN SEEN ALL THE HOUSE. have you?" Lucas asked, standing.

When Rae admitted she hadn't, he exclaimed, "Ah, let me show you the best part of the living room."

Despite the fact that was the one room she saw each time she ascended or descended the stairs, she walked with him from the lounge. He mentioned that his study, bath, and bedroom were behind the closed doors next to the lounge.

The foyer and staircase were separated only by space from the living room with its cathedral ceiling. A dim light burned on the wall near the foot of the stairs.

"Over here," Lucas said, without turning on another light. They stood looking out beyond the wide picture window where the mountainsides were dotted with tiny lights. The dark outline of mountain ranges seemed to stretch on forever, eventually fading into

71

the sky. Expecting Lucas to comment on the view, Rae was surprised at his question.

"Is it so important to you. Rae?"

"Is what so important?" she asked, studying Lucas's profile as he looked out toward the mountains.

"Attending church tomorrow—and Andy's lack of interest."

"I believe the most important thing in a person's life is commitment to Jesus Christ as personal Savior," she replied thoughtfully. "Church attendance is just one expression of that commitment. But I do think families should worship together. For example, I can't imagine being married to a man who doesn't share and understand my beliefs."

"Perhaps it's not an insurmountable problem," Lucas replied, and she felt his eyes search her face in the near darkness.

The subject shifted to the magnificent view before them.

"Asheville lies in that direction," Lucas said, pointing. "Not to be compared with Atlanta in size, of course, but it supplies our needs. In front of you is the Swannanoa Valley and, off to your left, is a little town called Black Mountain. . . . You're not looking," he said with surprise.

No, she had not looked at anything but his face since he had come to stand beside her. She could think of nothing but how she had felt in the early morning with his arms around her. Did he remember?

"I-I see only mountain peaks dotted with light. A whole blue ridge of them."

"I've looked at this view so many times," he laughed, "that I can see it with my eyes closed."

Suddenly brilliant light flooded the room.

"Wondered where you had gone," Andy was saying, striding across the floor toward them. His eyes held a strange gleam of triumph. "I just talked to Gran," he said, reaching for Rae's hands and holding them out in front of her. "She's delighted that we'll be going to church with her in the morning. She's eager to meet you, Rae."

"That's wonderful, Andy," Rae said sincerely.

"Now," Andy continued, "let's ride down to the camp. The lake is very romantic in the moonlight. But you'd better get a sweater. It'll be cool by the lake."

"Andy," she said when they neared the staircase, "Would you mind very much if we waited until tomorrow? I think I really did eat too much, and I feel I might be getting a headache."

At his look of disappointment, she almost changed her mind, but instinct told her she shouldn't. "I haven't unpacked," she explained. "After all, I don't have closets full of clothes like Mimi!" Her banter did little to lighten Andy's dark mood.

Reaching out, he placed a hand on her shoulder and the warmth she had detected earlier returned to his eyes. "I understand. There's plenty of time for us to see the lake—tomorrow, or even next week." He shrugged. "I really should spend this evening with Uncle Lucas, anyway. We have a lot of catching up to do."

Leaning forward, he touched his lips to hers. She was uncomfortably aware that Lucas was probably watching. But it was a very nice kiss, and Andy was really a very nice person.

After a moment, she moved back and smiled up at him. "Sleep well, Andy."

"See you in the morning," he said softly, then turned to rejoin his uncle.

Rae was pleasantly surprised on Sunday morning when Lucas appeared at the breakfast table and announced that he would drive them to church. Gran had planned to meet them there.

She was waiting for them in the foyer of the church. Rae was not surprised to find a tall, elegant, handsome woman who appeared twenty years younger than her seventy-plus years. Her silvery-white hair was beautifully coiffed, and her alert brown eyes held the speculativeness of Lucas's and the warmth of Andy's. Upon being introduced, Gran had immediately insisted that Rae call her Gran.

There was no time for conversation, but Rae felt comfortable sitting between Andy and Gran during the worship service.

After church, Gran got into the Lincoln with them to accompany them to lunch, and on the way back to Lucas's house, she told Rae about the historic sites in the area: The Biltmore House and Gardens, Vance's Birthplace, Thomas Wolfe's home, Carl Sandburg's Home, Mt. Mitchell, the Parkway.

"Stop!" cried Rae. "I'm overwhelmed just looking at the mountains. And now you tell me there's more!"

"Not to mention the boys' camp and the ski resorts," Andy teased.

Then Gran told her about the religious conference centers in the area, as well as several colleges. It all sounded fascinating, and Rae feared she would never be able to visit all those places in a single summer. It would be over all too soon. . . . But she mustn't think of that now.

During lunch, and afterward in the lounge, Rae learned that Gran was active in church work, served on several civic committees, and was athletic like her children and grandchildren. She had her own exercise room and remained a member of a tennis club. A live-in staff took care of things during her frequent travels.

"A woman friend travels with her," Lucas explained. "Gran has turned up at many of Andy's competitions, and at mine when I was more actively involved with sports."

"Well, Lucas. We Grants have to stay busy. We have a capacity for activity." Gran said. "Too many evenings spent alone can make one old before one's time.

"But that's enough about us. Let's hear about this fascinating girl." And she turned her full attention to Rae, who already felt a bond of kinship. "I'm so pleased to meet the young lady whom Mimi mentioned every time she wrote. It was a comfort knowing she had a friend she could speak of so highly, and one who wasn't afraid to lecture her when she needed it!"

Mimi pursed her mouth in a pout, but smiled at Rae.

"When my granddaughter wrote to me about you, I thought to myself: *Now there's a girl Mimi should bring home for all of us to meet*," Gran continued with a sparkle in her eye. "I just hope you have the good sense to take this adorable girl seriously, Andy," she said.

Andy perched on the arm of the couch, near Rae. "I told you last night, Gran. Rae means more to me every day, but she insists on time to think it over."

Only for a second could Rae meet the warmth and acceptance in Gran's eyes.

"I thought I detected a more serious note in your voice when you told me about her on the phone last night," Gran nodded. "I also sense that Rae is a fine young lady. Now, you win her over!"

Rae tried to smile with the others. Gran would not think well of her when she knew the truth. Such lying seemed to come so naturally with Andy. But Andy was a desperate young man. Now she felt herself being drawn deeper and deeper into his predicament. What had begun as a seemingly innocent suggestion was fast becoming a full-blown deception. What was worse, these people accepted her, liked her, wanted her to be part of their family.

"What is it, Rae?" Gran asked quietly.

"Oh—" Rae said, shaking her head—"my mind was somewhere else. I'm sorry."

Then Lucas was explaining for her. "Rae isn't as ready as we are to express her feelings, Gran. I think we embarrass her by speaking of personal matters."

"We *can* be rather blunt," Gran agreed.

But there had been a time when Rae was open about her feelings. That morning with Lucas. When he had conducted his cross-examination.

Monday morning began with Rae and Mimi running along the horse trails that wound around the camp area and down beside the lake that Mimi said covered six hundred acres. When the sun began to peek over the mountains that surrounded the camp area, Rae was reminded anew that God's handiwork could not be imitated by mere man. Gentle rays filtered through the cool morning air, moist with mist. The fragrance of honeysuckle, sweet and clean, delighted the senses, as they ran past rustic cabins, soccer fields,

76

tennis courts, and even a miniature golf course. But it was the modern gymnasium that intrigued Rae.

"The outside of the gym is used in teaching the fundamentals of beginning rock-climbing," Mimi explained.

There was a spot high above the camp where they could look down upon a pastoral scene with cattle grazing in the valley beneath, surrounded by sloping hills and mountain peaks, green, purple, and gray with haze at various levels.

The evergreens were alive with golden yellow-green fingers at the tips of each limb, stretching toward heaven to catch the sunlight.

Andy and Lucas were usually finishing their morning workout when Rae and Mimi were ready for theirs. The fully equipped exercise room was immense, encompassing the entire area beneath the first floor of the house.

The next few days passed quickly. While the two men spent much of their time on the campgrounds, Mimi and Rae were busy with exercise, swimming, tennis, shopping, and visiting some of the quaint little shops on Cherry Street in Black Mountain.

Suddenly it was Friday and time for Brent's party.

"Since the theme is Hawaiian, we have to dress the part," Mimi said, rummaging through her closets.

She brought out a brightly patterned silk dress for Rae and one of blue, green, and orange for herself. They donned low-heeled sandals before walking downstairs, where Andy waited in khaki pants and an exotic short-sleeved shirt. All thoughts of how handsome he was vanished the moment Lucas walked in from his bedroom and joined them in the foyer.

"Well, you look festive," Lucas said, smiling at them.

"Join us," Mimi invited. "It will be fun."

Lucas laughed. "I'm afraid I have other plans."

"A gourmet dinner?" Mimi teased. "In a romantic A-frame?"

Lucas gave her a noncommittal glance before saying, "Don't be out too late and—behave yourselves."

"If you will, Uncle Lucas," Mimi said mischievously.

He looked at his watch, said a hurried good-by and strode from the foyer.

Rae stared after him. "What was that about the A-frame?" she asked.

"Isobel's mountain hideaway," Mimi replied.

Rae suddenly realized how the three of them, dressed in their Hawaiian costumes, must have looked to Lucas—like children playing dress-up.

Upon arriving at Brent's, Rae discovered it was anything but a children's party. After winding their way up the mountain, Andy pulled the car to a stop in front of a magnificent two-story brick home with huge white columns.

Walking around to the back patio was like stepping into an Hawaiian travel poster. The three of them were immediately presented with fresh flower leis. A live musical group strummed musical instruments in accompaniment to native Hawaiian songs. Long tables were laden with festive decorations and elaborate foods, with centerpieces of pineapple and every conceivable kind of fruit.

"Brent does have a knack for giving a party," Mimi said brightly.

"It's fabulous!" Rae agreed. "I've never seen anything like this."

"We'll have one of our own when I get back from Paris," Mimi promised. "Oh, but I mustn't think of Paris. Tomorrow, Rae. Tomorrow I leave."

"Then stop thinking about it, Mimi," Rae said. "Here, have a . . . whatever this thing is."

They laughed and sampled the food. Rae determined to forget everything but the party and for the next few hours did just that, wondering briefly at only one point if Lucas were enjoying his evening with Isobel.

When Andy came up to her and led her away to a secluded part of the patio, she welcomed the retreat from the noisy guests—until he pulled her close. "After we take Mimi home, let's go somewhere, Rae. We haven't had any time alone." A rather desolate look appeared in his usually twinkling brown eyes.

Rae searched his face, and her heart went out to him. "Why don't you take me back to the house, Andy?" she asked kindly. "Then you can come back to the party and find another girl. I'm afraid I'm not very good company tonight."

"Rae," he whispered miserably. "I don't think you understand me. I don't want to be with just any girl. I want to be alone with you."

Rae lowered her eyes from his searching gaze.

"Look at me, Rae," he said and she lifted her eyes to his. "It's not what you think, Rae. I want to talk to you. I want to tell you my dreams and my plans. And I want to hear yours."

Rae was surprised at his earnestness as he continued, almost hesitantly. "I've never wanted that before, Rae. There's never been a girl who made me

79

think seriously about my future, and my personal actions, like you do. I'd like to think that if you knew me better, you'd see more than a-a playboy.'"

"Oh, Andy, who am I to judge?" Rae protested. "You haven't always made good decisions, but we all make mistakes."

"Not you," Andy replied with conviction. "You're sensible . . . and wise."

He didn't know that at this very moment she was struggling with a ridiculous girlhood fantasy that had come to life in the person of a man who had listened while she poured out her heart to him on a mountain-top. That was not at all sensible, or practical or wise.

But it would pass. Apparently, this was a common reaction of women to Lucas. As she became more accustomed to that mountain of a man, she would be better able to deal with her own emotions. And then . . . there was Andy. He had great potential. His skills were admirable. He was personally very attractive. Once she settled down to face reality again, she would accept these things about Andy with her heart as well as her head. It would just take a little time.

"I would like to know you better, Andy," Rae said truthfully. "But for now, I have a job to do. That's really why I'm here. I need to take things slowly this summer."

Andy looked up toward the starlit expanse of sky and sighed deeply. When he returned his gaze to Rae, the troubled look had disappeared. "Okay," he said, smiling. "Slow and easy it is."

It took another thirty minutes to say their good-bys, with Mimi promising to write from Paris. Rae could honestly tell Brent and his friends how much she enjoyed the delightful party.

It was when they returned to the house and entered the lounge that Mimi expressed her surprise to find Lucas sitting in the dimly lit room, watching TV.

"Uncle Lucas, you're home early," she said, hurrying over to stand by his chair where his lean frame was stretched out, his feet propped up on a stool. "Is everything all right?"

"Of course. Why shouldn't it be?"

"Did you and Isobel have a fight?"

"Isobel and I plan to spend the day together before she returns to Raleigh tomorrow evening. Now, does that sound like we've had a fight?"

"No," she admitted. "But you looked worried. You don't usually sit in the dark, watching TV."

"And you aren't usually home at this hour," he countered, looking from Mimi to Andy.

"I'm too excited about Paris to keep my mind on anything else for long," Mimi said, adding, "which reminds me—I have to finish packing." After a quick kiss on Lucas's cheek, she left the room.

"Did you enjoy the party?" Lucas asked Rae.

"Very much," she replied and looked at Andy. She wanted to give him an opening to return to the party. "But it *is* early."

"Maybe I'll watch TV with Uncle Lucas," he said.

"Fine," Lucas said. "Care to join us, Rae?"

"No, thanks," Rae replied. "I promised to help Mimi pack."

She started to turn but Andy reached for her arm and gently drew her to him, then placed a light kiss on her lips.

Rae stepped back immediately, expecting Lucas to be watching, but he seemed absorbed in finding a channel on TV. As Andy said good night, there was the sound of a lively commercial in the background. But it was Lucas's low, deep-throated, ''Good night, Ramona,'' that lodged in her consciousness.

CHAPTER 6

RAE GREETED SUNDAY MORNING with both anticipation and apprehension. She was excited about beginning her job at the camp, but wondered if she were equal to the challenge.

Mimi had insisted on arising before daybreak. Gran had arrived early. She and Mimi were already on their way to the airport. Lucas left for the campgrounds.

"Our lives won't be the same for the rest of the summer," Andy assured Rae, when it was time to head down the mountain toward the camp to begin a week of staff training and indoctrination, before the campers' arrival.

"Short cut," Andy explained while he drove down the steep, winding incline which led to the side of the gym and onto the gravel road in the center of camp. A short distance further, he parked the car and took her bag. They hiked up a winding path leading to a log cottage posted with a crudely carved sign reading: "Off Limits."

"It means what it says, too," Andy said emphatically. "None of the males are allowed up here." Rae suspected its authority had been challenged more than once.

A pleasant-looking woman in her mid-forties came out onto the deck as Andy and Rae set the luggage down. Andy introduced her as Marge, the director's wife.

"I've heard a lot about you from Lucas and Andy," she said. Marge's rather plain face, surrounded by very short brown curls, came alive when she smiled and her blue eyes expressed warmth. Rae liked her immediately.

"I'd better get myself down to the dining hall and meet the incoming staff before Lucas or Carl call for me over the PA system," Andy said, as if reluctant to leave, but he lifted his hand in parting, and hurried down the steep path. She watched as he got into the yellow car, turned it around and drove down to the dining hall. Her eyes swept the lake as she thought of the infamous diving board incident.

Marge stood beside her and pointed out her house, several yards from "Off Limits." A rustic mountain home with a shingled roof, it was situated in the center of camp. The house was almost obscured by lush green foliage and thick clumps of rhododendron, growing down the banks of a fast-flowing stream that ran in front of it. A bridge arched high above the stream, leading to the deck across the front of the house.

"That long modern building at the far end of the lake houses office space on the top floor and the infirmary on the lower floor. The nurses have quarters there during the summer. But we'll see it all later," Marge promised."

She opened the screen door and they stepped into the living room, furnished with utilitarian but comfortable furniture. "The fireplace is the only source of heat. Some evenings are quite cool, but you won't notice it most of the time. You'll be so tired, you'll simply fall into bed, she laughed."

"That's encouraging," Rae said and wrinkled her nose in mock dismay.

A doorway to the left led to Rae's bedroom. The furnishings were spartan in their simplicity—two cots, a dresser, and a chest of drawers. From the front window, she looked out upon the deck, then out toward the view of the lake and mountains beyond.

"You'll share your bedroom with the rifle instructor," Marge told her. At Rae's quick glance, Marge laughed. "*She's* an expert. Has won marksmanship awards for years. And she's only twenty-two. She was with us last year."

Two crafts instructors would room together in one of the other bedrooms; the crafts director, in the third.

"I'll take all of you on a complete tour this afternoon. Go ahead and get settled. I'll see you in the dining hall at noon."

The crafts director, who insisted upon being called by her first name, arrived first. Rae learned that Adele was a librarian at a private girls' college, had never married, and looked forward all year to leaving the heat of northern Illinois for the coolness of the western North Carolina mountains. "I've always been interested in crafts," she explained, "and these campers keep me young."

So that's her secret, Rae thought, for in spite of her

gray hair, her sparkling blue eyes reflected a lively spirit and love of life. "I would almost pay them to let me come here," she added, then jested, "but don't tell Lucas."

Rae was equally delighted when the crafts girls, Peggy and Linda, arrived. Peggy, an art major just finishing her junior year, was a tiny, cute brunette whose dimples accompanied a ready smile. Linda was a lovely girl from the Cherokee reservation. She would be teaching Indian crafts.

Leslie, the rifle instructor, was the last of Rae's cabinmates to arrive. Her red hair was her outstanding physical characteristic, followed closely by at least a million freckles. A tall, trim girl whose forceful personality was contrasted by warm brown eyes, Leslie was a college graduate who would begin officers' training school in the fall, to continue in the family military tradition.

Shortly before noon they walked down to the dining hall where the kitchen staff had set out, on long tables in the main part of the building, hamburgers with all the trimmings, crisp raw vegetables, and platters piled high with fresh locally-grown fruit.

Carl stood at the head of the line, restraining the hungry staff. When everyone was in line, Lucas went to the microphone and asked that they bow their heads. His prayer was a short, simple one, thanking God for the food, for the staff, and asking His guidance as they prepared to share their lives with young men.

After the "Amen," Rae regarded him long and seriously.

Lucas's acknowledgment of God was not just a ritual, but seemed to be as much a part of him as breathing. Though much about Lucas was a mystery to Rae, she sensed a deep religious conviction within him. She had felt it when they were on the mountain that first morning together, when he said he wanted a Christian girl for Andy, and when he admitted his own dependence upon God.

Considering all the things that appealed to her about Lucas, she realized he had never appealed to her as much as he did at this moment. Regardless of how much money a person had, or how physically attractive, a man was never taller, nor stronger, nor more intriguing, than when he admitted his need for God.

Rae turned and moved with the line to fill her plate. Her sudden elation was replaced by a sinking feeling. Her own faith in God would mean nothing to Lucas without a life to back it up. No matter how able she might prove herself to be on the job, she was sure that, when he learned the whole truth, he would not approve of her . . . not even for Andy.

Rae forced her mind from these unhappy thoughts and followed Marge and the others to the screened-in deck overlooking the lake. From this vantage point, they could see a huge colorful float near the diving station.

Marge explained that it was called the "blob." A boy could crawl out to the edge and sit on it. A counselor or several small campers would then jump off the diving board, land on the air-inflated blob, and the camper would fly up into the air, then come screaming down into the water, arms and legs waving wildly. "They all love it," she said.

After lunch, Lucas welcomed the staff, and introduced Carl and Marge, praising their efforts in directing the camp operation all year, in preparation for these few weeks during the summer.

When Lucas introduced Andy, he stressed his experience and training—leaving no doubt that Andy held his position as junior camp director, not because he was the nephew of the owner, but because of his own unique qualifications.

"This is a time for self-analysis and recommitment to the young men who are sent here from all over the world, to receive the best training and finest influence available. We're here to give them just that!"

How will I ever learn all these names? Rae wondered, as Carl asked the entire staff to stand and introduce themselves. Being able to state her own qualifications for being a part of such a select group gave her a good feeling. She was grateful she had the opportunity to speak of her father and saw some knowing nods, indicating that many of the staff knew of him.

After lunch, Marge took Rae and her cabinmates on a tour. She parked the Jeep in front of the long two-story office building. In the infirmary they met two of the nurses, Mable and Suzie, who assured them that at times those rooms would be filled to capacity. Sometimes a virus ran through the camp. There would be the inevitable scrapes, sprains, and bruises. And, occasionally, young campers would be stricken with homesickness.

"One little patient woke me up in the middle of the night," Suzie told them. "He looked so pitiful and, when I asked what was wrong, he said he couldn't sleep. Luckily, I had just the medicine," she said, laughing. "We keep ice cream in the refrigerator for just such emergencies."

Marge took them upstairs to the offices and introduced Ann, the executive secretary and receptionist. Before Ann could finish her greeting, the urgency of the phone demanded her attention.

Crossing the hallway, they entered another long room, where a bright smile from a very pretty face welcomed Marge and her entourage. Nina was introduced as the registrar, who processed the applications and kept all the information on each camper. "Her skills on the word processor are invaluable," Marge told them.

"And I'm Cindy," an attractive blond said when they turned her way. She began asking about each of them and Rae knew she was one of those rare, enviable persons whose warmth and vibrant personalities shone through immediately.

"Now let's get your summer uniforms," Marge said and they walked down the hallway to the clothing room where they met Laura, a young woman whose blue-gray eyes held a clear direct expression and her sweet smile gave the impression of early morning sunshine, fresh and pure.

Each of the girls was issued several sets of forest green shorts and khaki shirts. The shirts displayed a tennis player emblem on the left pocket, and the word *staff* embroidered above it. White socks also bore the emblem.

After leaving the office building, Marge drove them along the main road, which led to a front and back entrance. She pointed toward mountainsides dotted with cabins, each of which would accommodate eight to ten campers, a counselor, a junior counselor and a counselor-in-training. Nearer the lake were cottages for male staff and tribal directors.

Again it was the gym that fascinated Rae. Running the entire length of the huge building was storage space for all kinds of athletic equipment. One large room was devoted solely to gymnastic equipment.

"The gym is also used for church services on Sunday morning," Marge explained. "It's the only building large enough to accommodate all the campers at one time, except for the dining hall. Some of the campers are sons of noted Christian athletes, so Lucas often asks the fathers to speak. Even Billy Graham, who lives about fifteen minutes away, in Montreat, has spoken to our campers."

Soon Marge headed back toward "Off Limits." "You should get to bed early tonight," she suggested, handing each of them a packet. Later, when Rae looked over the papers, outlining the schedule during the next week of training and orientation, she had the feeling Marge had given good advice. The would be needing all the rest they could get.

After they turned out their lamps, Rae lay on the bunk nearest the front window, where she breathed deeply of the cool, moist night air and snuggled under warm blankets. All was quiet, except for the sound of crickets and insects claiming their right to the night. She could feel herself drifting off to sleep before she had finished her prayers.

CHAPTER 7

"WHAT WAS THAT?" exclaimed Rae, sitting up in bed. Outside her window and permeating her consciousness was the strident sound of a male voice singing, "Nothing could be finer than to be in Carolina in the morning!" accompanied by a loud trumpet.

With a groan, Leslie turned over. "I'm afraid that's our alarm clock for the entire summer!" she explained. "It's a tape they play over the PA system. And we will be warned that if anything happens to it, they have plenty of spares!"

Chuckling, Leslie flung aside her covers, and sat on the edge of her bunk.

Soon figures clad in green shorts and khaki shirts were jogging down the mountainsides toward the dining hall.

Lucas, attired in camp uniform like the others, welcomed everyone. After breakfast, the staff sat around the tables on the dining hall deck for Lucas's indoctrination, much of which included an explanation of the material in the packet Marge had given her.

"Our most obvious purpose," Lucas said, "is to provide the campers with a fun-filled, enjoyable three weeks. The campers will be divided by age: Junior camp, ages seven to eleven; senior camp, ages twelve to sixteen. After that, into tribes—Apaches, Seminoles, Cherokees, and Comanches. The younger, unskilled camper will strive—by improving some skills and learning others—to attain the rank of Brave and Pathfinder, the ultimate goal being Little Chief."

Normally a camper of thirteen, fourteen, or fifteen who had attended the camp for several years was ready to be tested for physical endurance and mental aptitude. Attitude was a major test, for a "Little Chief" must be gentle and helpful, as well as brave and strong.

"We will expose each camper to a variety of activities, and encourage him to excel in at least one area," Lucas continued. "Staff members must make written reports on each camper under their care. This will demand careful, meticulous evaluation."

Rae grew increasingly apprehensive as she listened to the stringent goals that demanded professionalism and organization. Every other staff member had submitted an application, with references that had been thoroughly checked. She had not. Each of them had been accepted with the clear understanding that he or she would be tested in a particular skill before acceptance was final. She hadn't had to pass a single test.

After this briefing, the staffers were told to get into their swimsuits and meet at the lake in fifteen minutes. Because of the many water sports—swimming, diving, canoeing, sailing, and life-saving—water safety was a must. Rae was perfectly at ease in this area, for she had always felt comfortable with water sports, and was especially skilled in diving. Even Lucas and Carl joined the others in the life-saving course.

Rae marveled at the way Lucas's great body glided through the water with such grace and ease. His muscular frame was surpassed only by that of David, a body-builder and one of the tribal directors.

Testing in all the other disciplines continued through Monday and Tuesday.

The staff gathered around the tennis courts to watch as the applicants for tennis instructor were carefully scrutinized during play. Though Andy was unexcelled, of course, the games provided excellent opportunity for the young men to demonstrate their skill, style, knowledge of the game, and attitude.

Rae's turn to demonstrate her expertise in gymnastics came on Tuesday morning. She would compete with two young men who had applied for a position in gymnastics.

"Could the guys go first?" Rae asked Andy.

"Sure," he said, after a moment's hesitation. His smile was warm, but she saw the questioning look in his eyes. She knew she had paled, for she felt that crazy case of jitters that often struck before competition. She must prove—to herself, as well as to Lucas, who insisted on the best in what he offered young campers—that she was a qualified instructor.

Rae watched from the sidelines as the two young men took their turns. They were good. Excellent, in fact. Her heart hammered, her palms grew moist, and she felt nauseous, in spite of the fact she had known better than to eat any breakfast.

Rae had spent some time in the gym the night before, practicing a few routines and testing the surface of the tumbling mat. She had decided to perform barefoot. The exact routine was familiar, one that she had used hundreds of times in competition, exhibitions, and classes.

Now her tape recorder, as much a part of her equipment as her warm-up suit and leotards, was ready on the sidelines. She joined in the enthusiastic applause for the young men, for it was well deserved. But she had been trained by Raymond Martin, and she was ready to demonstrate what he had taught her.

Were this a match of physical prowess alone, she knew she would fail, for the young men had displayed superior strength on the pommel horse and parallel bars. But her *gymnastics moderne* classes and their stringent routines had given her an undeniable edge.

She knew what she must do. She would not give less than her best. She would not simply display the correct movements, the results of many years of discipline and training, but she would give an exhibition. It would be a tribute to her father, and his years of tireless effort. She would draw upon the inner strength he always stressed.

And then Andy was calling her name—"Rae Martin."

Her father had always said, "When you see nothing but that vault, it's time to go." She stood, forcing the spectators from her mind, telling herself it was not Lucas she must please ultimately, but herself. She welcomed the intense surge of concentration.

Unconsciously she tugged at her leotards, brushed

at the hair that was already turning into ringlets, positioned her body, lifted her chin, felt the silence of an audience holding its breath, then stared at the horse until nothing else occupied her mind.

Her flight began. In an instant her body somersaulted in a tucked position, reaching the horse in a handstand. The next instant she completed the vault by a somersault identical to the first, then landed with a flourish, her back to the horse. The effort, concentration, and years of practice that had gone into the vaulting, was culminated almost as soon as it began.

Rae wiped her hands and her forehead, allowing herself time to catch her breath and decrease the rapid beating of her heart before she moved to the balance beam. In competition one slip on the balance beam could cost a medal or a career. While teaching the young campers, she would not have to follow all the rules, or perform the more difficult maneuvers. She would be expected only to demonstrate a knowledge of the basic tenets. However, for herself and her father, she intended to perform as if the gold medal were the prize.

She mounted by jumping from the springboard and landing on one foot at the end of the beam, keeping the other foot free and extending her arms. Her graceful movements incorporated the *moderne* technique. Strength, balance, agility, and personal innovation were evident as she performed her cat leap and turn, arabesque holding position, forward springs, aerial walkover, and, unrelentingly, a standing back somersault. She worked the entire beam, first supporting herself on her hands with one foot touching the beam, then kicked up to a handstand, turned 180 degrees to face the opposite direction, then executed a forward walkover and dismounted to land with her back to the beam.

With this part of the routine successfully completed, Rae couldn't allow the tension and pressure to leave her yet, but she could breathe a little easier. The uneven parallel bars gave her opportunity to exercise creativity in a way the vault and balance beam could not—these required much more rigid, meticulous movements. The asymmetric bars demanded a continuous movement, calling upon strength, agility, flexibility, and stamina developed through a regular program of exercise.

From a running position, Rae jumped from the springboard into the air, executed a 360-degree spin, grasped the low bar, circled over it forward, down and up again, supported herself above the bar, and dropped down. Then, hanging from the low bar with arms straight, she moved her legs forward in a piked position and propelled herself through a 180-degree turn upwards to grasp the high bar. With fluid grace she performed the swinging movements, suspension, and passage of her body between the bars. Finally, after circling up through a headstand on the high bar, she swung down, did a backward somersault and dismounted, facing the bars.

Rae's father always had told her to smile before she began her floorwork. She knew she had not failed her father this day, nor herself. Her broad smile reflected her appreciation of the audience's applause. Her next routine would be for them.

She could not relax completely yet. The floorwork, however, was her forté, and called for the kind of movements she had taught almost daily at the university for the past three years.

Standing at the edge of the floor mat, she lifted her arm. The music began. For the next minute and a half, her routine displayed the beauty and elegance of the female form as she combined artistic and gymnastic movements in her handsprings, somersaults, handstands, pirouette spins, and jumps.

Rae loved this, for it was the most aesthetically beautiful of the gymnastic events, providing graceful interludes between the tumbling movements. She perfectly performed a roundoff and a double back somersault, landed in a gymnast's graceful stance, then finalized the movements with a body wave by bringing her feet together, and standing on tiptoes with her head and shoulders back, knees and hips forward. After a quick bow, and lift of her arms, she ran from the floor.

Her radiant face, framed by damp curls, turned toward the audience that had risen to its feet spontaneously, applauding enthusiastically. That tribute was especially appreciated, for many of them were just as capable as she in their own particular skill.

She looked toward Lucas for approval, but he was talking to Carl and Andy, studying the clipboard in Andy's hand.

One by one, or in clusters, the staff began to leave the gym. Rae slipped into her warm-ups, then sat on a bench to put on her socks. When she saw the great hairy legs in front of her, she looked up.

"Raymond Martin would have been very proud of you today," Lucas said in a voice meant only for her ears.

CHAPTER 8

By Wednesday, the testing was complete, and final assignments were given. Rae would instruct gymnastics for both junior and senior camps, with the two young gymnasts assisting her, and would also take her turn on the waterfront.

The next several days were spent studying and absorbing camper applications. Rae felt she knew all the campers well, even before their arrival, for complete files were provided, along with photos.

Schedules and lists were made, revised, and approved. Plans were finalized concerning the skills that would be taught in beginner, intermediate, and advanced classes for both junior and senior campers.

By Saturday evening, after the intensive week of training, everyone was ready for a change of pace. Rae had been told that it was traditional for a girls' camp staff from another part of North Carolina, to travel to Lucas's camp for a square dance the night before opening day.

Rae had become so accustomed to seeing the green shorts and khaki shirts that it seemed strange now to be confronted with hillbillies dressed in jeans and western shirts. She had asked Andy to bring her a pair of jeans and a checkered shirt from the big house.

Lucas was standing near the door of the gym, greeting many of his guests for the evening, when Rae walked up.

"You'll be a converted hillbilly before the night's over," Lucas predicted. His friendly manner and mountain-man attire reminded her of the first morning they had spent together on the mountaintop.

"There's definitely a twang in the air," Rae laughed as she started to walk past him.

Lucas reached out and grabbed her arm, then steered her through the doorway. "The Mountain Creek Boys," he said, gesturing toward the small bluegrass band.

"Oh, look!" Rae pointed. "I didn't know Andy could do that!" She was intrigued to see Andy clogging with an attractive brunette from the girls' camp. There was toe-heel-toe tapping to the hip-slapping music of guitars, and those on the sidelines clapped to the beat, patting their feet and calling out a few "Ah-haws."

After the clogging exhibition, a square dance was announced. Andy and the brunette paired off, while others formed a circle.

"Now it's your turn," Lucas said, but Rae shook her head.

"I don't know how," she said regretfully.

"You don't need to know how. Just follow me." There was a challenge in his eyes.

Taking a deep breath, Rae squared her shoulders and walked to the circle with Lucas.

"All join hands," the call was given.

Lucas grabbed her left hand and, simultaneously, she felt her right one being grasped. She looked around into the smiling face of Hank, one of the tribal directors. Before she could object, the caller was singing out, "Circle left," and, for the next twenty minutes, she wasn't able to utter a word.

The circling was easy, but the calls confused her: "Texas star. Circle four. Swing that opposite girl. Now your own."

The only thing Rae understood was that when the caller said, "Now your own purty little gal," she was in Lucas's arms, then just as quickly was whisked away. It didn't take long for her to realize that no matter how confused she became, or how lost, Lucas always found her.

At one point, only briefly, Andy was her partner. "Having fun?" he asked.

She could only nod, fearful that by the time she answered, she would be handed off to another.

"Promenade around the ring, promenade that purty little thing." Two by two they circled, Lucas's arm around her shoulder, his hand holding her lifted one.

After the dance, Lucas was introducing Rae to the director of the girls' camp when Andy came up to claim her. When the next round began, he asked, "Want to try it?"

"I've had enough for a while," Rae said, laughing. "Go find yourself a good dancer and have some *real* fun."

Andy squeezed her hand and looked down into her eyes. A special gleam was there and his smile was sweet. "You're one girl in a million," he said, winked affectionately, then walked away. Andy found his clogging partner, and they joined the square dance circle.

Slipping through the doorway of the gym, Rae inhaled deeply of the brisk air. The coolness felt refreshing on her warm skin.

"You're apparently not the jealous type," Lucas said, joining her.

"It wouldn't change anything if I were," she replied noncommittally.

"No, I suppose not." Lucas's face wore a forbidding frown.

"I encouraged Andy to find a good partner," Rae explained. "After all, *you* danced with me."

"I'm part of the family," he countered.

Rae looked away. "Beautiful, isn't it? The stars are so bright."

"You should see them reflected on the lake," he said. "And tomorrow, we'll have about that many young men *in* the lake."

Rae laughed. "Noisier, I expect."

"Ah, quite!" He took her elbow. "Even noisier than that." He gestured toward the gym where the bluegrass music could be heard. They walked down the path, toward the lake.

"Is Isobel's son still ill?" Rae asked.

"No," Lucas replied, glancing toward her. "He's fine now."

"I'm surprised she isn't here tonight for the festivities."

Lucas grinned. "This kind of primitive exertion doesn't appeal to Isobel."

"Doesn't she like camp life? I mean, if you marry her, wouldn't she help you run the camp?"

Lucas's inquisitive glance made Rae wonder if she had become too personal. He gazed out into the distance before answering.

"Isobel appreciates what the camp does for her son. During the winter Kevin attends a private school. At summer camp we give him discipline, attention, and a sense of belonging. He needs that and Isobel knows it." Rae felt her face flush under his sudden scrutiny. "Do you think I would marry a woman because she might be an asset in my chosen field?"

Rae had to answer honestly. "No. I don't think you would."

"If you must insist upon knowing my deepest secrets, fair maiden," he said, taking her arm and leading her to a canoe tied up in a stall along the lakeshore, "then I shall whisk you away to yon faraway deserted island."

Laughing, Rae settled into the shaky craft. Lucas was a man of many moods. This was a side of him she had not seen before. "Yon island" was all of about fifty feet from the edge of the lake and not more than that in length, with two solitary trees on it.

"Now," he said, paddling on alternate sides of the canoe, "what were we talking about?"

"Why you never married," Rae reminded him. She felt strange being out on the lake alone with Lucas, beneath the stars. The music was so faint now that the sounds of night life were becoming more predominant. Her voice sounded strange to her own ears. "Why haven't you?"

Lucas looked surprised, then laughed low. "Ramona Martin, I have the sneaky feeling you're prying."

"Well, it works both ways," Rae said, lifting her chin. "You have asked me all sorts of questions. Do I not have the same privilege?"

"Yes," Lucas replied quickly, more serious than she thought he would be. "You're interested in Andy. His lifestyle and relatives are a part of him."

Rae stared down at her tennis shoes, then glanced up through lowered lashes. Lucas was still quite serious. "I think you're a girl who follows her heart instead of her head."

"You're wrong," she argued. "I'm like my father. I think things through before I make a decision . . . that is, generally." The absurdity of her claim struck her forcefully.

"Probably," he conceded. "It's just that the things that seem important to you are not the things most women in your position would consider priorities— financial security, social status, the right clothes. No," he spoke with conviction, "I believe you would be wondering if you could live with a man for a lifetime, bear his children, love him when he's at his worst." He paused, not expecting an answer.

Rae's voice was softly thoughtful. "During my mother's illness, my father and I were extremely close. There is something about the bond of suffering that draws people together. Because of her hospital expenses, we had financial difficulties, but no amount of money could have bought the love we shared. And our faith in God gave us strength to face her death. Then, when my father became ill, I learned all over again the sufficiency of God's grace. I suppose that's why, although I enjoy material things, I know there are more important things in life."

Lucas was silent, only occasionally stroking the

water with the paddle. He took the oar and laid it across the canoe in front of him. "I'm going to tell you something I've never told anyone," he said.

Part of Rae wanted to hear how he felt, what he thought, what was going on inside of him. Another part feared what he might say. Everything was still as she waited. There was no sound of music now, and even the night noises were being driven into the background by the sound of her own heart's beating in her temples. There seemed to exist only the two of them.

The thought flashed through Rae's mind that the lake looked different tonight. This morning it had been blue, clear, without a ripple on the surface, giving the appearance of polished glass, the reflection of the trees and the island and the dock perfectly reproduced. In the afternoon the lake had been a summer-leaf green. A light wind had stirred the surface much like one dips a spoon in frosting and lifts it, leaving slight indentations and peaks. Tonight it was a deep gray-blue, reflecting a myriad of brilliant stars. This would be the impression she would carry with her always.

When Lucas spoke, the sound of his voice, resonant and deep, lay gently on the still, starlight night. He mentioned having been acquainted with many women of many types, from many countries. "But there is a mountain in Switzerland that intrigues me," he added.

Rae looked at him quizzically.

"We're not compatible—that mountain and I," he continued. "She's treacherous, has thrown me many times, but I get up laughing, determined to accept her challenge. When I am skiing down that slope, I feel that I have made an important conquest if I reach bottom upright. Frankly, I rather like it when she wins.'' He looked at her then.

"And that's the kind of woman you want?'' Rae choked.

His laugh was light. "I used to think so. I often wondered if there was a woman out there for me who expected, even demanded, more of me than gliding smoothly along the slopes of life. But there always seemed to be a missing ingredient.''

"Do you know what was missing?'' Rae asked in a small voice.

"Of course,'' he replied immediately, that mocking expression on his face. "I thought I would fall in love. I had visions of such delight. As you seem to have done.''

Rae found his sarcastic tone irritating. "I wouldn't marry a man I *didn't* love,'' she assured him.

"Ah, love,'' Lucas said with amusement. "Is love some tangible thing, or some illusory fantasy? Is it not some figment of imagination one finds in a novel? Is it not wiser to be practical, sensible? Chasing love might be like chasing rainbows. Looking for that pot of gold that can never be found.''

"You mean you think I should consider how much I might gain financially when I marry?'' Rae asked, resenting his cynicism.

"I didn't say that,'' Lucas replied in a low voice. "I was merely suggesting that you consider your options.''

In that instant Rae realized that what often seemed like tender moments with Lucas turned out to be another of his attempts to explore her motives regarding Andy. And she had fallen for it every time.

105

That angered her. "So you no longer believe in love!" she fired.

Looking at her levelly, he lifted his eyebrows. "I know the mountain exists. Perhaps the woman does."

Rae shook her head in confusion. She did not understand him. Glancing over at him, she saw he was amused. It was difficult, if not impossible, to know when he was serious and when he was not.

He sighed. "As one grows older, however, the tendency is to be more of a realist, and less a romantic. I think I have come to the conclusion that such a woman does not exist . . . at least, for me. Perhaps I should settle for compatibility."

Rae watched as his jawline tensed. She almost regretted having been engaged in such a conversation, for now he seemed remote and sad.

"But there have been times, Ramona," he said softly, almost as if talking to himself, "when I have longed for a woman, not just to fill my arms, but to fill my heart. I think the most irresistible woman in the world would be one—" he spoke the words hesitantly, almost fearfully—"one who truly loved me."

His rugged profile seemed to be carved from the mountain itself. There was something touching about this man beneath whose steel and fire ran deep reservoirs of tenderness and longing, springing up like some subterranean stream from the heart of the mountain. He was a man who had everything, yet longed for something more.

"You have Isobel," Rae said quietly, and his gaze returned to her.

"Of course. And Isobel would fit in perfectly with my lifestyle."

"But you said she wouldn't care for camp life."

Now he looked at her as though she were a foolish child. The intimate sharing was over.

"This is only a small part of my life, Ramona," he explained. "The camp is very important to me, but I also have a winter resort in North Carolina and one in Switzerland. And perhaps you aren't aware of my line of sports equipment. Isobel would be greatly admired in those circles."

"You seemed to so enjoy preparing for camp, the boys, the square dance," Rae said weakly, remembering his vitality and verve, his hearty laughter. He was a part of these mountains, this culture.

"I can live without it," he replied tersely. "All this will be Andy's someday. You would be an ideal partner to work alongside him. You're good for him, Ramona."

To cover her sudden discomfort, she sought a subject that would take his mind off her relationship with Andy. "It has occurred to me that it seems a shame that only young men will be here to take advantage of the expert skills of your staff. Have you ever considered making the camp coed?"

"You must be a mindreader," Lucas replied immediately. "I've even thought of discussing the possibility with you. It would take a very special kind of woman to direct it. With your background, skills, and Christian commitment, Rae, parents would admire and respect you. They would feel comfortable sending their girls to such a camp."

"I wasn't speaking of myself, Lucas," Rae protested quickly.

His smile was warm and beautiful. "But I believe you are that very special person who could make it successful.'' He reached for the oar and began to maneuver the small craft toward the island.

Rae felt the rising panic within. Her thoughts were in turmoil. She wanted to blurt out hers and Andy's deception, free herself of the weight of guilt before things went any further.

Strange, when she had agreed to accompany Andy to North Carolina, it hadn't seemed so complicated. She had justified his silly scheme in her own mind by telling herself she was helping a young man who had made a foolish mistake. She had even thought she might be a good influence on him. But now it had grown all out of proportion. Confession would ease her conscience. She could then obtain Lucas's forgiveness, and try to set a genuine Christian example for the camp.

But the timing was all wrong. Beginning tomorrow, each of them faced tremendous responsibilities. Lucas had emphasized that the campers were their top priority for the summer. Her confession would cause division among Lucas, Andy, and herself. Rae would just have to suffer silently—for the sake of all of them.

Feeling trapped in a web of deceit, Rae lifted her hand to her head, then looked for any sign of distraction from her thoughts.

''Oh, look!'' she exclaimed as a fish broke the surface of the water further out. She leaned over just as Lucas swung the oar.

''Watch it!'' he cautioned abruptly, but too late. The canoe was tipping and, before she could regain her balance, she was plunging headlong into the water.

Lucas released the oar and followed her. For an

embarrassing moment, both of them flailed about, reaching for the paddle.

"Oh, Lucas!" Rae sputtered away the lake water. "What an awkward thing for me to do!"

"I quite agree," he said, attempting to right the canoe.

Rae swam around to the other side. "We'll never get back into this thing," she wailed.

"We'll just have to drag it back to shore. And to think," Lucas said with amusement, "we were almost stranded on a deserted island."

"Almost," Rae repeated, trying to imitate his joking manner, then added incredulously, "Am I doing all the work?"

"It would appear so," he replied. "Why don't you relax and try walking?"

"Walking?" Rae stammered, then realized they had reached shallow water.

They both laughed. After Lucas secured the canoe, he came over to where Rae stood shivering. "Your clothes are at the Haven, aren't they?" he asked.

"Everything except my camp uniforms."

"Let's jog up there," he suggested. "We can change, then I'd like to discuss some plans with you."

When they neared the gym, Lucas spied a counselor. "Tim," he called, "would you please find Andy and tell him that Rae and I have gone up to the Haven?"

"Sure," Tim replied, a grin spreading across his face at the sight of the soggy couple. "He was inside just a minute ago."

"Let's go," Lucas said to Rae and they began to jog up the road by the gym, their tennis shoes squishing with every step.

After reaching the house, Lucas and Rae sat on the top step of the first deck to remove their shoes and socks. "Sorry I ruined your evening," Rae said apologetically.

"Ruined my evening?" Lucas asked, as if the idea were preposterous.

"You probably weren't ready to come home yet."

"If I hadn't been," he replied, pulling off his socks, "I would have stayed there and drip-dried."

"I'm glad you're not angry," she said sincerely, grateful for his lenient attitude.

"I will admit I hadn't planned to swim in my jeans," he said, taking her shoes and his own. He set them side by side at the edge of the deck, with the wet socks on top. Then he came back and drew her up by her hands. "But the evening was not a total loss," he assured. His voice grew soft. "I enjoy teaching you things."

Rae looked up at him, his dark eyes shadowed as he bent his head toward hers. "I like teaching a city girl how to adapt to our mountain ways. How to square dance. How not to rock a boat."

Rae told herself Lucas was being very kind, trying to make light of their misadventure. Perhaps that intense look on his face was her imagination. But the feel of his warm breath against her cheek was all too real. "Fortunate is the man who will have the privilege of teaching you," he added, "everything."

Rae longed to tell him she wished that he might be that man, but his next words seemed to contradict any such possibility. "I believe he's here now," he said as tires screeched against the gravel on the driveway.

A concerned Andy was bounding up the steps. He

stopped suddenly, taking in their wet clothing and bare feet at a glance.

"This time it was not a glass of water, but an entire lake," Lucas laughed. "She dunked me—right out of the canoe!"

CHAPTER 9

"UNCLE LUCAS TELLS ME you have some terrific ideas about including girls in the camp program," said Andy after Rae entered the lounge, clad in a warm sweater and slacks. In her haste to shower and change, she had not bothered to dry her hair, and it curled in tight ringlets about her head.

"I don't know anything about camping except what I've learned this week. And that knowledge hasn't been proven yet," she shrugged, "So I'm not about to tell you how to run a girls' camp," she said adamantly.

"You look terrific, Rae," Andy said admiringly, "even without your hair fixed, and with your nose all shiny."

"Thanks, Andy," she smiled and sat down beside him on the couch. "But I really don't know how I can help you, so flattery will get you nowhere."

"We don't expect that much, Rae,"Lucas assured her, handing her a cup of steaming hot chocolate which she accepted gratefully. "We just want your opinion on a few things. There were times when I had hopes of Mimi's taking an interest in this venture, but I've abandoned that hope. I've been waiting until I felt the time was right. Perhaps, now, it is."

Lucas walked over to a file cabinet near his desk and removed a folder, then returned to the easy chair he had pulled up to the coffee table, across from Rae and Andy. He moved the tray aside and laid the folder on the table.

"This is the area at the back of the camp, beyond Marge's and Carl's house, where cabins could be built. And this mountain here," he said, pointing to a plat of his property, "could be leveled and a new gym built there. Do you think the girls' gym should be separate from the boys'?" he asked Rae.

"I think so," she asserted. "It would be good to have some interaction between the boys and girls—even competition—but their training should be separate. They would want to impress each other with their skills, but I don't think they would be comfortable together while in the learning process."

To prove her point, Rae related some experiences she had had as a child at church camp. "They should be together for meals, though," she smiled, remembering.

"Then I would need to extend the dining hall," Lucas mused, looking at Andy for his opinion.

"There's plenty of room to expand," Andy said. "And even for extending the deck out over the lake. How many girls should be enrolled?"

"What do you think, Rae?" Lucas asked.

Rae felt he knew exactly what he would do, but wanted to hear her answer. "If," she began, emphasizing the conditional stipulation, "if it were my decision, I would limit the number of girls. I would employ staff with exceptional skills, like you have for the boys' camp, and accept only girls who are interested in athletics. It's so important to train them properly when they're young. Some of the girls in my classes at the university had learned habits that were almost impossible to overcome, and hampered their technique."

"A small group of girls, seriously interested in athletics," Lucas nodded in approval. "That would diminish some of the supervision problems that have concerned me."

"It would be a great service to young girls," Rae suggested. "A real ministry—if handled properly."

"Yes," Lucas agreed readily. "If we get the right person to direct it." He handed them blueprints of the cabins, and an area marked off for a swimming pool. "We could make the swimming pool Olympic size," he said.

"Oh, to be young again!" Rae exclaimed. "I'd like to be one of those campers myself."

"I'm sure Uncle Lucas will let you sign up, Rae," Andy laughed, reaching for her hand.

"I've kept you two long enough," Lucas said, gathering up his blueprints. "You probably want to get back to the square dance."

"Shall we?" Andy asked Rae, and she felt he was eager to return to the campgrounds.

"It's fine with me," she said agreeably.

"Thanks for your opinions and suggestions," Lucas said, closing the folder and standing. "And Andy," he continued seriously, "although you have done a good job with the camp in the past, I detect a new sense of direction and a more positive attitude about you this season. I'm confident this will be our finest summer yet."

"Rae has a lot to do with that, Uncle Lucas." Andy smiled down at her. "I'm beginning to understand what you meant when you talked to me about taking life and relationships more seriously. Maybe it just takes that special person to make a guy realize it."

Lucas nodded. "I want you to know something else, Andy. Whenever you're ready to settle down and take over the running of the camp, I'm ready to begin releasing more responsibilities to you. And Rae," he continued, looking deep into her eyes, "I consider it a privilege having you on our staff. I can well picture your heading up the girls' camp. Think it over."

Lucas's acceptance and approval of her was not only reflected in his words, but in his eyes. Rae felt lost in his poignant gaze for a moment. How pleased he seemed to be in believing she and Andy might marry.

"Lucas," she began helplessly, and his questioning gaze invited her to continue. But she felt Andy's hand grip her shoulder and she recognized his signal that a confession at this moment would destroy the confidence his uncle had just expressed in them. "Good night, Lucas," she said.

Andy steered her out the door before she could reconsider.

"How could you possibly put on such a blatant display of hypocrisy, Andy?" she blurted out angrily when they were in the car. "It's bad enough to know we're playing this deceitful game, but you're behaving as if everything is settled between us. That's going too far!"

Andy was undaunted by her anger, and tenderly touched her lips with a finger. "I'll tell you all about that in about three weeks. A date?"

"Definitely!" Rae assured. She knew she must try to come to terms with her emotional conflict. But she couldn't think about that now—not with three weeks of camping just ahead.

Sunday morning dawned bright and clear. Although registration was scheduled from one to five o'clock, campers were piling from cars, and buses full of noisy boys were arriving from the airport even before the eleven o'clock church service scheduled in the gym.

It was a memorable moment when nearly one hundred staff members, campers, and guests joined in the singing of several favorite hymns before Chuck, one of the tribal directors who would return to the seminary in the fall, sang a solo in his beautiful baritone voice.

The famed area evangelist spoke on the wonder of the body, the temple of God. He praised Lucas for his ministry to the physical growth of young men and emphasized the even more important need for spiritual growth, which could be accomplished by an acceptance of Jesus Christ as one's personal Saviour, then a daily exercise of the Lord's teachings.

After the service, everyone was invited to share in the picnic lunch to be eaten outdoors, since part of the dining hall was being used for registration lines.

Rae was to assist on the waterfront. Each camper had to be tested in order to determine if he belonged in a beginner, intermediate, or advanced swim class.

She knew they'd have to give time for lunch to settle before allowing the boys into the water, but by one-thirty she was clad in her swimsuit and a floppy hat that Tim had found to keep her nose from turning into a beet in the hot sun. On her clipboard was an alphabetical list on which to rate the swimmers.

Time passed quickly and by four o'clock over half the expected three hundred campers from all over the United States and abroad had completed the test. Standing, Rae stretched, feeling the tightness of her muscles from having sat so long observing and evaluating the style, speed, stamina, and confidence of young men as they swam.

"Take a break, Rae," Tim urged. "You deserve it."

"I do need to stretch my muscles," Rae replied and turned.

It was the woman's platinum hair that caught her attention first. Holding tightly to Lucas's hand was a little boy with hair the same startling shade.

So intent was she on the newcomers that Rae scarcely noticed the camper who walked up to her on the dock. Vaguely she saw what appeared to be a rope around his neck and was about to tell him he couldn't go into the water with it. .

"Will you hold my snake while I swim?" he asked innocently, extending his arm, the slithery creature coiled tightly around it.

Rae shrieked, and was forced to exhibit some of her fanciest diving technique.

Realization of what had happened was instantaneous. Everyone was laughing, and Johnny reached for her hand to help her back up on the dock.

Tim was telling the stricken camper that he couldn't

keep the snake. He must either put it back where he found it, or take it to the nature center.

Rae's heart went out to the little fellow. Careful not to get too close, she apologized for screaming. "I just didn't expect to meet him," she explained. "It's really a very . . . nice . . . snake. I hope I didn't scare him."

"Oh," the camper said with a grin, "he'll be all right. I'll just put him back. You think he'd like that better than the nature center?"

"I think so," Rae replied and he smiled with relief.

There was no longer any way to avoid the trio waiting at the edge of the dock. She was dripping wet, had lost her hat, her hair was in tight ringlets, and she could feel the heat in her face.

"I . . . he had a . . . " she began, but found herself stammering under Lucas's amused expression, and the cool, tolerant look on Isobel's placid face.

"We saw," Lucas assured. "Congratulations. You've been fully indoctrinated into camp life. I want you to meet Kevin."

Feeling uncomfortable in the presence of the immaculately groomed Isobel, Rae knelt in front of Kevin, who was still clinging to Lucas's hand.

"I've heard a lot about you, Kevin. Are you feeling better?"

"I've heard about you, too," he said. Unexpectedly he leaned forward. "I know how you feel," he whispered.

"You don't like snakes either?" she asked.

Frowning, he shook his head. "But if you let anybody know, they'll try to scare you all the time— on purpose!"

"Then I'd better act brave," she said with wide eyes. "You want to be brave with me?"

He straightened his frail shoulders and nodded.

"Bobby," Rae called, "may I go with you to put the snake back? Kevin's going along to protect me."

"Sure," Bobby replied and walked over to them. "Girls are scared of snakes," he confided to Kevin.

Isobel's thin smile was Rae's only clue that the woman was pleased with the attention Rae was giving her son, but Lucas winked his approval. She and the two little boys and the snake headed off down the path.

After Kevin and Bobby were tested, Kevin was breathless.

"Can I be in intermediate?" he asked, his eyes large and pleading, his new friend beside him. "Bobby and me can be buddies if we both make it."

There was no doubt that Bobby qualified for the more advanced rank, but Kevin was another matter. Yet Rae felt it was important to Kevin. He was a very lovable child, but doubted that he made friends readily.

"You got very tired, Kevin," she reminded him kindly.

"That's because I've been sick. But I'm O.K. now. Honest! Ask Tim. I was in beginners last year, and he said I might could move up this year."

Knowing determination could play a major part in one's accomplishments, she relented. "I'll talk to Tim about it and we'll see."

"All right!" Kevin shouted and grinned over at Bobby.

By Tuesday, the camp was settling into the routine it would follow for three weeks: Breakfast, at eight o'clock; classes, beginning at nine.

Kevin was in Rae's beginner gymnastics class, and just as she had feared, he was not well coordinated and hadn't the strength for many of the routines. Due to his agility, she suspected he might be good at tumbling, so she encouraged him to try. It was soon apparent that what Kevin needed most was a personal touch and, since there were only ten boys in this class, she was grateful that she and her assistants could give him the individual attention he craved.

Lucas put in an appearance during her first beginner class.

"You're doing wonders with Kevin. Thanks. There's more to camp life than athletic training. I appreciate your sensitivity." He looked at his watch with a grimace. "Hey! I've got to go. See you around." And he was on his way.

Rae turned her attention to the boy with the mop of pale hair. He was an adorable child, eagerly reaching out for affection. Yes, Kevin needed a father—a father like Lucas, she admitted ruefully.

Almost before she knew it, the beginner class was over and the intermediate had taken its place, demanding more than training in balancing, tumbling, handstands, and cartwheels. Coaching the advanced class required all her discipline and skill, for the young men had already learned techniques that needed to be refined. Here, however, they did not utilize music which she had found so valuable in her teaching at the university, for it provided rhythm, an aid in timing.

During the remainder of the week Rae felt that her head never quite touched the pillow before the now familiar strains of "Nothing could be. . ." were calling her to a new day.

Like a spring, she bolted from under the covers, so welcomed during the cool nights, and leaned over onto the windowsill to read the Bible and meditate. Each day the view was different—sometimes clear, sometimes with a smoky haze encircling or resting upon the lush green mountain peaks. Inhaling deeply of the fresh morning air, she thanked God for the beauty He had created and for the joy of sharing it with others.

It was not until Sunday that Rae had a day off. After attending church services in the gym and eating in the dining hall, she went with Andy and Carl to see what was being done to the mountain behind the boys' camp.

"That's where the new gym will be," Carl said, pointing to a portion of mountain that had been leveled and cleared, readying it for the foundation.

"Lucas mentioned naming the gym after your father, Rae," Andy told her. "It will be known as the Raymond Martin Gym."

Rae was speechless. Finally she managed to ask, "Lucas would do that? For me? For my father?"

Emotion welled up in her eyes. She was hardly aware of Andy's arm circling her waist. They walked over the mountainside, discussing the cabins, the spot for the pool, the plans for the dining hall. What had been only marks on paper that night in Lucas's study were becoming a reality before their eyes.

She longed to ask Lucas about it, to express her appreciation for his tribute to her father, but there was not the opportunity during the next week, nor the next. Rae was aware, reluctantly, that the first session was rapidly coming to a close.

In the evening as she sat on the deck of "Off Limits" or in her room by the window, working on evaluations or contemplating three hundred "little Indians" who were scattered about the mountainsides, she was amazed at how much learning and fun could be packed into three weeks.

Suddenly it was Sunday afternoon again and first session was over. Rae stood in front of the dining hall saying good-by to the many campers who promised to write to her.

When Kevin came by, his handshake was surprisingly firm. Rae felt her eyes misting and there was a catch in her throat when she told him good-by. In case she wanted to write, he gave her his address in Raleigh, then added that he would be staying with his grandparents in Asheville during the following week.

Isobel, too, seemed strangely moved when she came to collect Kevin and his belongings. "Thank you for what you've done for my son," she said, before the icy veil of reserve dropped over her eyes once more. Only once did they brighten as she looked past Rae. "I'll see you tonight, darling," she called in her soft Southern drawl.

Rae didn't bother to turn. There was only one person to whom Isobel could be speaking.

"Mimi called early this morning," Lucas said, to Rae when Isobel and Kevin had left. "It appears there's to be a wedding. I suspected that would happen when she left for Paris."

"Oh, she loves Pierre so much!" Rae turned then to

face Lucas. "I'm happy for her. But I didn't know you knew."

"I make it my business to know everything about my wards," he retorted. "Mimi's grandparents in Paris are well aware of her actions, and keep me informed."

Rae detected a certain reticence. "You don't approve?"

"From all I hear, Pierre is a fine man. And you're right. Mimi does love him very much. Incidentally," he said, changing the subject. "You will stay at the Haven this coming week. Most of the staff will be gone until the weekend. Then we begin again."

"Is it all right if I come to the Haven tomorrow?" she asked. "Andy is taking me out tonight, then later I have to finish my reports for Carl. So, I would like to stay at 'Off Limits' tonight."

"Fine," he said and added, "Gran will also be coming to the Haven tomorrow to spend the week with us."

Only Selma was at the Haven when Rae and Andy arrived there to dress for the evening. After taking a leisurely bath, Rae put on a chocolate-colored dress that fell in soft folds to just below her knees. She fastened gold earrings at her ear lobes and a thin gold chain around her neck, then stepped into high heels. Her skin had acquired a bronze sheen during the past three weeks, and her cheeks glowed with natural color. Only a little green eyeshadow was needed to enhance the color of her eyes. Her hair had taken on the effect of spun gold which her father had loved, and her soft, full lips shimmered faintly with a touch of gloss.

Feeling ready for a night out, she hurried to the

lounge, expecting Andy to be waiting. She stopped short. Lucas stood inside the doorway, dressed in evening clothes.

"You look lovely," he said and then, as if to explain his comment, added quickly, "Our costumes are quite different from that of the past few weeks."

But Rae knew that did not explain why she didn't seem able to take her eyes from him. His physical attraction was undeniable, but even more than that were the wonderful inner qualities he had displayed during the past month. She had seen it in all he did— in his expressed purpose for the camp, his involvement with the staff, his concern for a fatherless boy, his kindness to a . . . fatherless woman.

"Lucas," she said, remembering, "the new gym. Have you really considered naming it after my father?"

"I intend to," he replied. "Your father made a significant contribution to the sports world. Through his daughter, that contribution has been extended to my camp. His name will not be forgotten. I'll make certain of that."

"Why?" she whispered. Rae did not mind that his dark eyes were probing hers, as if seeking out her innermost thoughts. Her gratitude was something she wanted him to see.

"Why?" he repeated, then she felt some kind of withdrawal in him as his eyes left her face. "I would do anything within reason for my family. And you're likely soon to be a part of it. . . . Enjoy your evening," he said, looking away from her to speak to Andy, who just entered the room.

Andy had reserved a table by a window on the twelfth floor of Grosvenors. Here they could look out above the traffic of Asheville, beyond the city lights, to the dark peaks forming a protective background against a graying sky.

The silence was not uncomfortable as they smiled across the intimate table for two. Rae sensed that this would be a significant evening. The very ambience of the elegant restaurant suggested intimacy and sharing.

After their order was given, Rae looked out where the land touched the sky. "The stars are shining," she said softly. "I sincerely doubt there is a more beautiful place in the world than the Smoky Mountains."

Andy made no comment and Rae turned to look at him. He was twisting his glass thoughtfully.

"There is one place that appeals to me more," he said, and she knew he wanted to talk about it. "There's a little village in Switzerland, near Uncle Lucas's ski resort. It's quaint and charming. There's a certain chalet on the side of a mountain where you can look out and see for miles. When the area is covered with snow, there's nothing else like it anywhere."

Rae was surprised at Andy's declaration of love for Switzerland. He seemed to be trying to convince her, pausing only long enough for their food to be set before them, tasting it, and making complimentary remarks.

"There is a sports shop on a main street in that small town. It's for sale. A friend and I have talked about buying it and seeing if we can make a go of it."

"I love hearing about your dreams, Andy," she assured him, sharing his excitement. "Have you told Lucas?"

"That's the only problem," he confessed. "You've seen how Uncle Lucas is so eager to turn the camp over to me. He has trained me, set his hopes on me. I've tried, but I don't seem able to tell him that I would turn down a probable lifetime security with the camp for a shop in Switzerland that might fold at any minute. It really doesn't sound very responsible, does it?"

"You've proved you can be responsible, Andy. I've seen it this summer. So has Lucas. And I think your plans are commendable. Lucas would understand your wanting to do something on your own. I don't think he wants to force you to run the camp. He's just offering it to you."

"When I go, Rae," he said with determination, "I want to take you with me. As my wife. Surely you know I've fallen in love with you."

Did she know? There had been indications, but it hadn't really registered. They had been so busy during the past weeks. Her gaze slowly turned from Andy's waiting eyes and toward the sky, twinkling in its blanket of stars.

It occurred to her that her acceptance would be the perfect solution to almost all her difficulties. Lucas would not have to wait any longer to marry Isobel. Kevin could have his much-needed father. She and Mimi could be life-time friends. She and Andy could be—compatible.

But slowly creeping into those thoughts was something more akin to the dark peaks beyond—so unmovable, mysterious, foreboding.

"I'm not asking for an answer right now," Andy said across the silence. Just think about it. Hey, this is delicious steak. How's yours?"

"Perfect. Just perfect."

"And the pianist?"

She looked toward the dark corner. "Excellent." Then it dawned upon her that Andy was trying to put her at ease, telling her to relax. "It's really a wonderful evening, Andy," she smiled then, with genuine pleasure.

"There can be many more like them, Rae."

Yes, she knew. An exciting, romantic life could exist for the two of them. Here, or in Switzerland. A lifetime of being loved by Andy should be all, and more, that a woman could ask for.

When Andy parked below "Off Limits" later that night, Rae did not protest when he pulled her gently toward him and pressed his lips against hers in a lingering kiss. Wishing with all her heart that she was in love with him, Rae allowed herself to be wanted, to be desired, to be loved, until his mouth became more demanding.

When she gently pushed him away, Andy sighed heavily. "Rae," he said seriously, "there have been many things I've wanted to hang onto rather than settle down. But now, I would give them all up . . . for you. You will think about what I've said, won't you?"

"Yes, Andy. I will," she promised. She would try, with all her might, to think about what Andy had said.

Too tired to stay awake, Rae postponed her thinking and her work. The following morning was spent in finalizing evaluations and making reports. It was late afternoon before Marge drove her and her few belongings up to the Haven.

Seeing no one about, Rae went upstairs to the room she had occupied a month before. After a leisurely bubble bath she slipped into shorts, a thin summer blouse, and sandals. Rae put away her few personal items, then felt the sudden change in the air. She walked over to the window where the wind was restlessly stirring the curtains.

The late afternoon sky, heavy with clouds, looked as if it had deliberately waited until after the campers left before spilling its contents. The blue sky became gray, then almost black, as the rain began to pelt the house and deck with heavy drops. The heavens rolled and rumbled. Bright flashes of light revealed the downpour upon the foliage. Gutters could not hold it all and splashed upon the deck. Sheets of lightning lit up the world, while streaks sizzled down the mountainsides.

Rae was unaware that the bedroom door had opened wider, admitting a shadowy figure, until Lucas spoke nearby, "Rae, are you frightened?"

"Frightened?" she asked, turning around.

"The electricity is out," he explained. "Andy is bringing lamps."

Rae shrugged. "I didn't know. I hadn't tried to turn them on."

He came to stand beside her. "That doesn't sound like a city girl talking."

One moment the lightning bathed his tall, athletic frame in light, its strange reflection in his eyes; the next moment, he was clothed in semi-darkness. The air was so still in the room that she parted her lips for breath and gazed up at the darkened figure, the face turned toward her, the man not touching her, yet seeming to. She was not sure if the vibration she was feeling was from the thunder or from somewhere deep inside.

"I don't think my training as an athlete prepared me for city life," she said in a strained voice. "I simply tolerated it. I seem to be awakening here in this primitive country, and I don't quite understand it."

Rae was allowed only intermittent glimpses of his inscrutable face, with the lightening gleaming in his eyes, his face shimmering with silver streaks, then fading into the darkness again.

"But you aren't afraid."

"Maybe I *am* afraid," she said, her voice a whisper.

The world was so strange with the turmoil outside contrasting with the breathless calm inside the room.

"The fear of a storm is a healthy respect," Lucas said. "Even those trees which have weathered many storms and have grown strong and tall and seem indestructible can be reduced to shreds in a storm like this. No matter how mature, they are quite defenseless against the forces of nature."

"Defenseless," Rae breathed as his face came nearer, suddenly illuminated, and a tremendous rumble of thunder set the hills to quivering. The crash was that of a cymbal.

In response Rae clung to him, trembling, as vulnerable as the time-worn trees. All sorts of things could happen—in a storm like this. All sorts of things, and they were happening—in her mind, in her soul, in her heart.

CHAPTER 10

Rae opened her eyes to a yellow glow in the doorway. It was Andy, carrying a lighted oil lamp.

She stood frozen, immobile, conscious only that she and Lucas had been silhouetted against the window. She could not be sure that Lucas had stepped back before Andy appeared.

"Storms can be frightening," he was saying, as if in explanation. "Go with Andy, Ramona. I'll close the window."

Andy left the lamp on a hall table for Lucas. In silence, with Rae's hand on his arm, they walked down the stairs and into the kitchen. Another oil lamp burned in the center of the table, and others, casting crazy shadows on the walls, flickered around the room.

Lucas entered the kitchen, saying, "Gran called before the phones went out. She felt it best not to venture out in the storm."

Andy nodded, but Rae had the distinct feeling his

mind was not on what Lucas was saying. Even Selma's cold supper of ham, green salad, applesauce, and spice cake was eaten without enthusiasm.

Rae tried to keep her mind on the few comments made about previous storms and the damage they had done. Even Selma, apparently concerned, kept looking out the kitchen window.

After they had finished eating, she came over to clear the table.

Finally, Andy broke the silence. "I'm not sure how to say this," he began and Rae's heart seemed to stop beating.

"If you have something to say, Andy," Lucas said quietly, his voice carefully detached, "then out with it. I can't read your mind."

Rae braced herself.

Nervously Andy ran his hand through his thick brown hair. "I had a letter from Celeste today." He raised troubled eyes to his uncle after looking apologetically at Rae. "She knows the camp schedule and that I have this week off. She's coming here."

"I thought that was over and done," Lucas said bitingly, his eyes sparking in disapproval.

"It is as far as I'm concerned," Andy assured him, glancing again at Rae, then adding helplessly. "But she didn't ask. She just announced that she was coming. And," he cleared his throat, "her flight arrives in the morning. She might be expecting to stay here."

Lucas leaned away from the table. Dark shadows clouded his face. "So what do you do now, Andy?"

"I don't know," Andy admitted helplessly.

Lucas leaned forward again, clenching his fists beneath his chin. His dark eyes flashed in the lamplight. "Perhaps we could allow Celeste to stay awhile, Andy. Rae could go to Gran's, or to the cabin, or even stay with Marge and . . ."

Andy's sudden intake of breath and look of incredulity halted Lucas's words. "Uncle Lucas," he said, "Don't you understand?" His voice rose to a higher pitch. "You can't do that. Rae is the woman I'm going to marry."

Rae felt certain Andy would shrink beneath his uncle's stare. Finally, Lucas rose from the chair. "I'm just trying to determine what you're made of. I thought you might be forgetting what you have in this girl here."

He nodded toward Rae who quickly rose from her chair and walked over to the window above the sink. She could hear Andy's reply. "I have no intention of forgetting, Uncle Lucas."

"How many times do I have to tell you?" Rae blurted. "You can't discuss me as if—as if—I'm a tossup. Heads, somebody wins. Tails, somebody loses." Hot tears sprang to her eyes. "And *I've* made up my mind about *everything*! Andy, I will not . . . "

Before she could finish her declaration, Andy was on his feet. Striding over to her, he put his hands on her shoulders soothingly. "I know you're upset, Rae. But let's not discuss it further tonight. You'll see once Celeste gets here that she means nothing to me. There's no one else for me now but you. Don't forget that for a minute."

His grip relaxed, but his eyes in the dimly lit room were pleading for her not to say anything more.

With a sense of resignation, Rae nodded.

"Please, Rae, please be patient with me," he whispered. "This will soon be over."

132

Lucas interrupted. "I'm going to check on Gran," he said, "and stop by the camp."

"Would you like me to do it, Lucas?" Andy offered.

"No. That won't be necessary."

"May I go, too?" Rae asked. She wasn't sure why she said it. It just suddenly seemed necessary to get away from Andy. And to escape the unbearable tension in this room.

"In this storm?" was Andy's immediate response.

"It's the best one I've ever seen," she retorted and looked toward Lucas for his reaction.

"It seems to have subsided a little," he commented, looking out the window.

"Do you mind if I go?" she asked again in a small voice.

"There's a raincoat of Mimi's hanging on the pantry door, I believe," Lucas said in reply and walked across the room, returning with the coat and putting it around her shoulders. Rae drew it close to her and the two walked toward the doorway.

"We'll be back in a little while," Lucas said. "Gran might return with us."

The evening was unreal. Rae felt a strange calm, a lull inside, steeled against the storm raging around them. It had eased some, the rumbling distant, the flashes of lightning more infrequent and farther away. The wind wasn't as strong.

After Lucas headed the Jeep down the drive, Rae said, "Perhaps we should have asked Andy to come along."

"He has a lot of thinking to do," Lucas snorted in derision.

Nothing else was said as the Jeep bounced down

the gravel road, flanked by swiftly flowing streams, swollen from the downpour. Lucas stopped outside the dining hall, where a faint glow shone from the windows. Staff members were gathered around, playing games, eating, and talking.

Catching sight of the newcomers, Marge called, "Great night for ducks! Why don't you stay? It isn't often we can *really* rough it!" Her gesture included the oil lanterns and the cozy fire.

Carl told Lucas that the electric company had found the reason for the power outage and assured him the lines should be back in service within a few hours.

After climbing back into the Jeep, Rae drew her knees up on the seat and stared at Lucas, who was watching the road, apparently unaware of her fixed gaze.

When he looked in her direction, she shifted her eyes to the wet streets. Although visibility was greatly diminished on the Interstate, Rae did not feel frightened; rather, invigorated. She was content to entrust herself to the big man with the sure knowledge of the road ahead.

When they pulled up in front of Gran's house, she met them at the door.

"I thought you'd come by," she said. "But I've told you it isn't necessary to keep such an eagle eye on me. I won't break—or melt."

Lucas laughed. "It's such a beautiful night that we couldn't resist the urge to go joy-riding."

"Well, come in before you drown," she invited, opening the door wider.

"We're not staying, Gran. Would you like to go back with us?"

"Not on a night like this!" Gran protested. "But

maybe Rae would like to stay here for the night. Would you, dear?"

She shook her head quickly but looked away from Gran and out toward the rain. "Thank you, but no," she said quietly. "I like the rain."

Perhaps it was her imagination but there seemed to be only the sound of rain splashing against the hood of the plastic raincoat. Reaching up, she pulled it off her head, allowing the rain to drench her hair.

"Is Andy in the jeep?" Gran asked, craning her neck to peer into the vehicle.

"No. And you should know that we're having a guest tomorrow. One of Andy's former girl friends is dropping in. So be prepared for anything."

"That doesn't sound sensible to me, Lucas."

"Nor to me," he replied and changed the subject. "I suppose we'll see you in the morning."

"I'll be there early. Now you two take care."

"We will, Gran. Good night."

The violence of the storm was past, a steady downpour continuing. Lucas concentrated on the roads, particularly the one up the mountain to his house. "These roads can be tricky," he said.

"If we get stuck, we'll just get out and walk."

"I think you'd like that," he said, glancing over at her, then had to do some fancy maneuvering when looking back at the road.

"Keep your eyes on the road," Rae bantered.

"I'll try," he said, and managed until he pulled the Jeep to a stop and switched off the lights.

When Rae stepped down from the Jeep, her raincoat slipped from her shoulders. Since her shorts and blouse were soaked, she folded the coat over her arm as they walked up the steps onto the deck.

"You're all wet," Lucas said, not taking his eyes from her. "There are towels in the pantry."

The oil-burning lamp cast a lonely circle of light on the kitchen table and ceiling. With the brightening of the sky, a faint natural light shone in through the kitchen window. They squished across the tile floor to the pantry door.

"There's a hook inside the door," Lucas said, opening it. Rae could not see it, but reached.

"Here, let me." Rae felt his hand touching hers and, then his body pressing lightly against hers. His bulk blocked out the light through the pantry door, thrusting her world into total darkness. Or maybe her eyes were closed and she had ceased to breathe. There was a suffocation, a wonderful, terrible inability to comprehend any other world outside this vacuum created by Lucas's nearness.

One or both of them moved. His hard lips groaned, then found hers. Emotion coursed through her body as his hand slid up and carressed her neck. There was a storm going on inside her, a flood about to break loose. "Ramona, Ramona," he whispered huskily against her ear, her lips. Then his warm breath was labored against her cheek.

"Oh, Lucas, I've never felt like this before," Rae whispered against his lips, standing on tiptoes, never wanting to leave the magic circle of his arms. Looking up into his face, barely outlined by the dim light, she whispered the truth she had long refused to acknowledge. "I care for you so much, Lucas." She wanted him to know her heart belonged to him.

But before she could say she loved him, he was speaking. "And we all care for *you*. Andy loves you.

Mimi and Gran care. And," his voice was shaky as he added, "and I."

Then he moved her away from him. Rae could not even lift her head. She was wrong when she had assumed she could take such a dive and survive. She felt as if she had drowned. "I'm wet," she whispered. "And cold. Let me . . . go." She did not think she could ever face him again.

"Ramona," he said. The way he spoke her name sounded so helpless, then he began plummeting her self-esteem. "Please forgive me. I can't explain it. Perhaps I'm just a man who has not led a disciplined-enough life. And tonight you were especially vulnerable, knowing that Andy's former girl-friend is on her way here. Can you? Will you forgive me?"

She was nodding. "Yes," was all she could whisper. Then she reminded herself not to panic. It was like losing a major competition. On second thought, she had not even been in the running. She had not stood a chance with Lucas from the very beginning.

Surely he could not see her tears in the darkness. Please, not that too. Then his arm lay gently across her shoulders. There was nothing to do but fall into step beside him.

At the kitchen table he stopped, took the lamp and handed it to her. Whatever words he attempted to speak were not forthcoming. He sank into a kitchen chair, leaned forward with his elbows on the table, his face in his hands. Rae quickly left the room.

CHAPTER 11

AFTER REMOVING HER WET CLOTHING, Rae dried herself and slipped into a gown, then lay in the darkness, listening to the distant mumblings of the abated storm. She would like to drift with those clouds, sail off into the night, disappear somewhere.

The wonder of Lucas's arms around her, the hope that he was beginning to care for her as she did for him was shattered when he drew away. He regretted his actions and had asked for her forgiveness.

Trying to force the humiliating scene far from her mind, her thoughts turned to how far they had all come since that afternoon in her kitchen in Atlanta when it seemed her part in this charade was simply to allow Andy to say he wanted to marry her. It had seemed to be Andy's dilemma ultimately. Not anyone else's.

But it wasn't that way at all. This family was so closely knit. What affected one, affected all. The Scripture verse came back to haunt her that what one sows, one surely reaps. Now, the pretense would be extended further. Even to Celeste.

Lucas must have a very low opinion of her, she surmised, throwing herself at him that way in the pantry. And it was not the first time! There was that morning on the deck. He must wonder what kind of girl invited his kisses while she was supposed to be Andy's girl. When he knew she and Andy had played such a game with him, his scorn would be unbearable. She was torn between wanting Lucas to know the total truth while another part of her wished he never had to find out.

Her muddled mind was invaded by sporadic snatches of sleep, but when nature's limbs stretched toward the gentle rays of morning sun, her own lay listless. While feathery white clouds skipped gaily along the blue ridges outside her window, her own inner longings were suppressed by a smoky, gray haze.

Tossing the covers aside, she willed her body to move. The back of her neck ached with tension. Perhaps later she would go to the exercise room and work the kinks out of her body. She wished there were such a room for the mind and the soul.

After brushing her teeth and washing her face, she slipped into shorts and a shirt. Last night's wet clothing still lay in a heap in the bathtub. There wasn't much she could do with her hair without washing it, so she gave up and let it curl in wayward ringlets. Circles beneath her eyes indicated her inner turmoil.

Hearing voices, she walked to the window, then stepped back and sat on the edge of the bed. On the deck, Lucas and Andy were conversing with Gran. A few minutes later, Rae peeked out to see the two men retreating down the steps. Gran was lounging in a chair.

When she thought it safe, Rae went downstairs. "Good morning," she greeted Gran, who was apparently enjoying the fresh coolness of the morning.

"It's always so clean and clear after a heavy rain," Gran said. Rae returned her smile. She walked over to the edge of the deck. The scent of earth and pine perfumed the air.

She turned when asked where she would like her breakfast served. "Eat out here if you like," Gran suggested. "Bring some coffee for me, Nancy, please."

Rae was grateful for Gran's suggestion. It would be impossible to choke down a single bite in the kitchen. She sat in a chair by a table, near Gran.

"I hope you aren't coming down with a cold, Rae, after being out in that downpour."

Rae shook her head. "I don't think so." Her hand went to her hair. "I haven't done anything to myself yet."

"It's charming, dear. No, I just meant that you seem a little tired, that's all." Gran smiled. "This week should be for relaxing. There are still three hectic ones coming up at camp."

Rae thanked Nancy when she brought her breakfast. It looked good, but she wasn't very hungry. Feeling the need for black coffee, she reached for the cup.

Gran pulled her chair closer to the table. "There was quite a discussion going on when I arrived this morning." The older woman sipped her coffee. Rae stirred the scrambled eggs with a fork. Selma had prepared them with mushrooms—a gourmet treat. Still, her appetite was not tempted.

"I hope you aren't letting this disturb you too much, Rae."

She looked away from Gran's worried eyes, wishing she could tell her that it was not Celeste's arrival that was upsetting her. Instead, she forced a bite of food into her mouth.

"But of course you're upset," Gran added with a sigh. "Everyone in this household is. That's why Lucas has ordered Andy to bring Celeste here."

"Ordered?" Rae gasped, almost choking on the bite of food.

Gran nodded. "He's greatly perturbed with Andy. I don't think Lucas slept last night, either."

Rae reached for her orange juice. "Can't he just let Andy handle this?" she asked weakly.

"That's what Andy asked him. He said he was going to tell Celeste that he loves you, and put her on the next plane to Florida." At Rae's quick glance, Gran continued. "But Lucas said he had tried that before. That Andy was supposed to have settled the matter with Celeste over a month ago, but hadn't. Since Andy doesn't seem able to handle his life maturely, Lucas is taking matters into his own hands."

Rae was almost afraid to ask. "What is he going to do?"

"Lucas said that Andy is not going to play his philandering games with you," Gran said, looking out where the gentle breeze stirred the leaves of a tree. Then she glanced back at Rae, with a strange light in her eyes. "He's going to demand that Andy make his

141

intentions clear concerning you and Celeste, right in front of everyone."

"Everyone?" Rae questioned, afraid of the answer.

Gran's concern was apparent as she replied slowly. "Yes. He had planned to discuss Mimi's engagement with the family tonight at dinner. And, Isobel mentioned that she wanted to discuss Kevin with you since you had spent so much time with him at camp. So. . ."

Rae pushed the plate away and stood. "I can't," she said, shaking her head. "I can't sit at a dinner table across from," she choked back the sobs before adding, "everyone. It's just impossible."

"My dear," Gran said in a whisper. "We're all on your side."

Yes, she knew. Lucas had told her how they all cared for her. A sob escaped her throat. "I'm sorry," was all she could say before turning from Gran's sympathetic eyes and running across the deck to the safety of her room.

The tears had dried on her face when, over an hour later, an knock sounded on her bedroom door. Andy called her name and pleaded for her to let him in.

"Just a minute," she said, went to the bathroom to douse her face with cold water, then returned to sit on the edge of the bed. "Come in," she called.

"Gran told me how this is upsetting you," Andy said, pulling up a chair. Misery was written on his face. "Believe me, Rae. I never intended to hurt you in any way."

"I know that, Andy. No more than I intended to hurt your family. But they will be when they know what we've done."

He took her hands in his. "Rae, I know I was wrong. But we don't have to confess our mistakes to my family. You and I can deal with it ourselves, can't we?"

A ray of hope sounded in his voice. "You see," he continued, "what started out as a lie has become the truth. I have asked you to marry me. You did say you would think about it. So why do they have to know?"

"Andy," she said quietly, "I hope I will never be able to deceive people and feel good about it, or explain it away. Even if they never knew, *I* would know. I can never have peace of mind, or seek God's forgiveness, without telling your family and asking their forgiveness."

"I knew you'd say something like that," Andy sighed. "Can you be there tonight when I tell the truth in front of Lucas and Celeste?"

"Truth, Andy?"

"That I love you and want to marry you."

Her heart went out to him, for she knew how it felt to have love rejected. She opened her mouth to protest, but he stood to leave, with a look of determination in the set of his jaw.

"I don't want Celeste here at the house today. I'm going to drive her around the area and convince her that she and I have no future together. And tonight," he promised, "everyone will know for certain where I stand with you."

"Please don't, Andy," she said, but he ignored her plea, leaving her to stare at a closed door.

Rae awakened with a new determination. She had slipped from a balance beam upon occasion, failed in an attempt to grasp an asymmetric bar, even during

143

competition. But she had forced herself to continue while knowing her final score would be lowered.

She reminded herself that a team member in gymnastics pushes herself, even after an embarrassing fumble, to keep on for the ultimate good of the entire group. That's what she must do tonight. There was the ultimate good of the camp to consider, as well as Andy's feelings.

But there was one thing she could not do. And that was to sit at the dinner table and pretend that she was not in love with Lucas Grant.

When Nancy came to her room to say the family was ready to dine, Rae truthfully replied that she wasn't feeling well and would not join them for dinner. A short while later, Nancy returned with a tray, exemplary of Selma's culinary expertise.

Rae forced herself to eat a little, then pushed it aside. She decided not to sit in her bedroom and wait to be summoned.

She stood at the window in the shadowed living room, watching the sun go down behind distant peaks, when the sound of voices traveled toward her from the hallway. Turning, she saw a young woman between Isobel and Andy.

Andy must have lost the courage to tell Celeste he didn't love her, Rae surmised. Otherwise the young woman could not be holding onto his arm like that, while engaging Isobel in such lively conversation. Celeste was not the picture of a girl whose heart had recently been broken.

They walked into the lounge, followed by Lucas and Gran, talking quietly. Gran entered, but Lucas stopped at the doorway.

He glanced toward the staircase, then, as if sensing

her presence, turned and looked in her direction. He was silhouetted against the light and Rae stood in near darkness, yet she felt his eyes on her. *How*, she wondered, beginning to move, *can it be easier to walk a balance beam than to cross that expanse of floor?*

Neither spoke as she passed him, and the other voices soon died away.

Andy, looking uncomfortable, walked forward with Celeste, who was still holding onto his arm possessively. After a quick appraisal, Rae realized the brunette's dark eyes held the expression of a confident woman prepared to do battle with her rival.

If sheer outer beauty of dress, face, and figure enticed a man to fall in love, then Isobel and Celeste were unsurpassed. They had dressed elegantly for dinner in a mountain mansion, and their beauty complemented the attractive men in that room.

In contrast, Rae had chosen a simple cotton dress, enhanced only by a single strand of pearls and pearl drops at her ears.

She was not inhibited by the girl's vivacious beauty, nor by the trace of hostility in her voice after they were introduced.

"Rae?" Celeste questioned skeptically. "A boy's name?"

Rae's smile was genuine. Celeste couldn't be more than twenty-one and reminded Rae of some college students she had known who were still young enough to believe that verbal combat was the only method of dealing with a rival.

"I was named Ramona, for my father, whose name was Raymond," Rae explained. "I like it, but it doesn't compare with yours. Celeste is a beautiful name, and you're a very beautiful girl."

145

Celeste's mumbled thank you quickly covered her momentary confusion.

Not wanting any undue attention, Rae looked around and found a place to sit between Gran and Isobel. Celeste began to remind Andy about the good times they had together, as they sat on a couch opposite Rae. Seeing a shadowy figure move behind them, Rae was grateful when Isobel mentioned Kevin.

"He was like a different child," Isobel said with genuine pleasure, "when he showed me the certificate he received for tumbling."

"A little encouragement can go a long way in building a child's confidence," Rae replied, and suggested some exercises that would increase Kevin's physical strength.

A glance across the way told Rae that Andy was well aware of his uncle's presence behind him, and he was talking in low tones to Celeste. Just when there seemed to be nothing else for Rae and Isobel to say, Celeste's voice was heard asking, "Don't you still love me a little, Andy?"

One word penetrated the hushed silence that fell upon the group. It was the first time Lucas had spoken. "Andy!" he said, and the sound carried all the force of a speeding arrow, heading straight for the bull's-eye.

Andy drew a ragged breath and Rae know what courage it must take to stand and surrender to his grim-faced uncle's staunch demands.

"I told her, Uncle Lucas," Andy said and looked down at Celeste. "I told Celeste that our relationship is over, and" he looked at Rae then. "I love Rae and have asked her to be my wife."

Rae quickly looked down, embarrassed for the girl. Gran reached over to pat her hand.

"Celeste," Isobel said, rising from the couch and smiling at the girl, "why don't you come home with me tonight? Tomorrow we can shop in some of those quaint little places I mentioned during dinner."

Celeste stood, threw a defiant glance in Lucas's direction as if he were some kind of villain, then said, "I'll call you tomorrow, Andy."

She walked swiftly toward the door, followed by Isobel, who had just proved what an asset she could be to Lucas, in helping to ease a difficult situation. She looked around. "We can find our way out," she said, smiling sweetly at Lucas.

After they left, Rae felt she must make her escape. "I think I'll go to my room," she said, but Andy detained her.

"Not yet, Rae," he said with determination, striding over and sitting on the edge of the couch opposite her. "I don't want you carrying this burden any longer." His voice softened. "I only want to make you happy." He looked around at his uncle. "It's time you knew the truth."

"The truth?" Lucas asked, as if that were something all the philosophers in the world had sought, but to no avail.

Andy told the entire story. From beginning to end. He took the full blame, explaining that Rae was only the victim of his persuasion. He told of her reluctance to go along with the scheme initially, and her need of a job.

"I'm sorry, Uncle Lucas. It seemed the easiest way to get myself out of this situation with Celeste."

Lucas had leaned forward with his elbow on his

knee and his hand on his forehead, moving his head from side to side as if he could not believe what he was hearing.

Rae couldn't look at Gran, sitting so still beside her. She could not bear to see the hurt and disappointment on that dear face.

'Andy,'' Rae said after a long pause, ''stop blaming yourself. Your family knows that I make my own decisions. And I made a wrong one. I'm sorry, too.'' She shook her head in remorse. Tears stung her eyes. ''I'm sorry I allowed you to accept me for something I'm not. I'm so sorry.''

Lucas's words cut like a spear. ''You two think that's all there is to it? Confess? Receive instant forgiveness?''

It was difficult to face his expression of fury, but she looked at him resolutely. ''No, I don't. I know I've failed each of you. I know you thought I was that fine Christian girl you wanted for Andy. You certainly can't think that of me any longer. It didn't seem so wrong in the beginning. But now, I'm so ashamed.''

Andy halted her words of apology. ''Rae, it's over,'' he said. ''We aren't going to be spanked like naughty children. We've said we're sorry. There's no longer any pretense.''

''That's right, Andy,'' she replied miserably. ''And I can't pretend that I'm going to marry you. I'm not, Andy. You have to understand that. I can't marry you.'' She hated what she was doing. How could she tell Andy she didn't love him? Humiliate him further? Break his spirit? She could only repeat, ''I can't.''

''You don't mean that, Rae, '' Andy soothed. ''You're understandably upset. You'll see. Tomor-

148

row, everything will be different. Let's just drop the subject for now."

"I agree," Lucas said and stood as if the matter were ended. "We will get through the next three weeks of camping. Then Mimi will be here and we will all sit down and discuss this in a reasonable manner."

Rae jumped up. She couldn't bear his treating her like a wayward child. "No, Lucas," she said. "I'm not your ward to be told what to say and when to say it. And whether or not you believe it, I'm not going to discuss this further."

"Believe you?" Lucas asked. "How can I know when to believe you, or what to believe? I asked both of you about your relationship. And each time I came away convinced of the probability of your engagement."

He inhaled deeply, but wasn't finished. "And now I'm supposed to believe Andy is in love, but you won't marry him? And you don't want to discuss it reasonably. Is there more? Are there other deceptions you are covering up?"

"Uncle Lucas," Andy said and stood. "Don't talk to her like that."

Rae felt she couldn't stand any more. "Both of you stop this. You don't have to argue over me! I'm leaving!"

"Please, Rae. Please don't," Andy pleaded.'

Defiantly she turned to Lucas. "I'm leaving!"

"You signed a contract to work at the camp for the full season," he reminded her, strangely calm. "It's only half over. The going gets tough, and you want to quit. Is this really Raymond Martin's daughter I'm hearing?"

The fight went out of her. She could only stare

down at the floor. "He would be as ashamed of me as I am of myself," she replied, her voice a whisper. "I'll stay. But I can't stay here. I don't belong at the Haven. I'm going to pack my bags now and go down to the campgrounds with the rest of the staff."

"Wait until morning, Rae," Andy suggested.

"No." She shook her head. "I have to go tonight."

Lucas did not protest and she knew he felt that was best. She was just an employee now, not a prospective member of the family.

Rae turned to Gran. "I'm sorry," she said, choking back her tears, then hurried from the room.

She had packed everything she had brought from Atlanta and set the bags in the hallway. Lucas appeared to drive her to the campgrounds.

On the short jeep trip to "Off Limits," Lucas's tone was that of an employer talking with his employee. He simply informed her what to expect and what would be expected of her during the week between the camp sessions.

He parked in front of "Off Limits" and took her bags up. Adele appeared long enough to speak and see Lucas setting the bags inside the screen door.

"Ramona, can I trust you to stay until the end of camping season?" he asked and the quietness of his voice surprised her.

She looked up at him and his seemed to be the only face in the world, the only eyes, as she stared at him and nodded.

"And to think," he said so low she almost didn't hear. "That slope in Switzerland broke only my leg."

He turned and left the deck. Rae looked after him for a long time, wondering why he made that remark. Had he meant she had done worse? He probably meant she had broken his trust in her. Perhaps his faith in human nature. Those things were more important to him than human limbs and bones.

CHAPTER 12

HOW SIMPLE THINGS MIGHT HAVE BEEN had Rae fallen in love with Andy rather than Lucas, she thought. But she hadn't. And in spite of the ache in her heart, and the belief that neither Gran nor Lucas could ever again respect her, she felt a great burden had been lifted now that the truth was known.

Rae was grateful for the stringent demands of the second session's youngsters, who needed and wanted her undivided attention, and left her exhausted at the end of each day.

She saw Andy and Lucas only briefly. Andy dropped by during some of the morning junior classes; Lucas, in the afternoon, each of them seeming determined to concentrate only on camp business.

One evening, when most of the campers had gone with their counselors to Cherokee to see the play, "Unto These Hills," she and Andy walked by the lake. The sky was star-spangled; the evening, mild and clear.

"Would you reconsider our relationship, Rae?" he asked seriously.

"I'm sorry, Andy. But I can't."

He sighed deeply. "I've been thinking some more about Switzerland."

"Tell Lucas," she prompted.

"I can't just yet. I've pulled too many surprises on him recently. But, Rae," he said, taking her hands in his, "I do love you."

"Thank you, Andy," she said softly. She knew it was true, but he probably loved Switzerland better, and she was glad.

Lucas did not approach her, unless it was a matter of business. Through Carl she learned that Lucas was aware of her interest in the plans for the girls' camp, and heartily approved.

Time moved so swiftly. It seemed she had just watched the sun go down, only to rise to the sound of "Nothing . . ."

Nothing! The word echoed in her mind. *Nothing* from Lucas ever. Not his respect. Nor his admiration. Nor his love.

She went for one last swim the morning the young men left the camp. After leaving the lake, she tied the terry cloth wrap around her, then spotted Lucas sitting in a wrought-iron chair near the dock. She had to pass him in order to get to the cabin. What could she say?

He stood when she came near. "Beautiful morning," he said. She stopped, nodded, and looked around as if seeing it for the first time.

"It's over," he said, but she was already aware of that. This was her last day. She could leave anytime. Her paycheck would be ready.

"There's something special about working with young men who have such potential for accomplishment," he said.

Rae nodded. Next year someone would be working with the girls in the same capacity. She had offered some valuable suggestions. It would be a good program.

"I've loved the work," she could say honestly. "It isn't just work, but a sharing of one's self."

"You have a feeling for it," Lucas said, then looked out over the lake and mountainsides. "I really expected you and Andy to be working together this time next year."

"I'm sorry I disappointed you," she said, but avoided his gaze, staring down at her bare feet on the wooden boards.

"It seems the other way around," he countered. "I believe we disappointed *you*. We couldn't offer you the things you find important. And you aren't swayed by money or outward appearances."

Not swayed by outward appearances? Not swayed by the personal magnetism of a man whose appearance was superb—breathtaking as a tall pine, glorious as a vivid sunset, calming as a gentle breeze on a misty morning, sweet as a ripple on a lake, fragile as a blossom on a shrub, strong as a mighty oak, all-encompassing as a leafy maple? Not swayed? Of course not. Her rapid heartbeat was a figment of her imagination; the sudden quickening of her pulse when he came near was a fantasy; the deep longing for his arms about her and his lips on hers was not real at all. It was all a mistake—another mistake.

She could only lower her head, hoping he would not see what was in her eyes: the truth, the longing, the desperation, the misery. The silence seemed interminable.

"Do you have plans?" he was asking.

She shook her head.

"Would you do me a favor?"

"I'll try."

"Go with Gran to pick up Mimi at the airport." She looked at him. "When?"

"This afternoon."

Rae's eyes brightened and her smile was genuine. "Of course. I'd love to."

The smile he gave her in return was beautiful and the sunlight gleamed in his dark brown eyes. "At least there's one member of our family who hasn't disappointed you," and added, "yet. She would never understand if you didn't have dinner with us to share her excitement over the engagement. Then we'll talk."

Rae stiffened. What was there to talk about? She had already expressed her caring for him, but either he didn't believe it or disregarded it.

"I have nothing more to say, Lucas, and I really don't feel like socializing."

"Only the family will be there—Andy, Mimi, Gran, you, and me. As I've explained before, Ramona. All of us . . ."

She couldn't bear to hear him say *that* again. "All right. I'll be there." She turned quickly and began walking toward the cabin.

He is relentless, she thought. He would not rest until everyone was completely debilitated with their sense of guilt for having deceived him. She would attempt to bear one more night of humiliation.

On the way to the airport Gran commented on the

155

oppressive heat. "We can expect a few days like this toward the end of July," Gran explained as if apologizing because it was not another of many perfect days. Rae wore a cool sundress and had slipped her feet into high-heeled sandals, grateful that her tanned, smooth legs did not require hose.

It was a wonderful reunion. Mimi's face shone almost as brightly as the huge diamond on her finger. Love certainly agreed with her.

Rae felt that Andy and Lucas were as glad as she that dinner consisted of a full-course meal of Pierre. Tonight she was here just as Mimi's friend. It was good not to have to pretend anything with Andy, who was quieter than usual, but obviously pleased for Mimi.

After dinner they settled in the lounge with coffee while Mimi discussed her plans. She wanted to return to Paris, marry Pierre right away, and complete her last year of college at the university where he taught. She might even decide to teach there until she and Pierre were ready to have children.

"You would be satisfied settling down like that, Mimi?" Lucas asked seriously. "You've never really worked. I probably failed you there."

"I've settled down for three years with my studies, Uncle Lucas, and I didn't do too badly. Study is very confining. Oh, Uncle Lucas! I could live in a tent with Pierre and be utterly content! I would slave for him!"

Lucas was nodding. "Of course you could. For a month or so."

"Oh, it's going to be fun, Uncle Lucas. He has a nice home near campus. We would be at the same school every day. But," she teased, "if you feel we would be too confined, you could, for a wedding present, give us a little place on the Rivera where we could escape on weekends.''

"A little place on the Rivera," he repeated. "Just like that.''

"Oh, Uncle Lucas," Mimi said, running to him and putting both arms around his waist. "I love him so much. He'll take care of me. He loves me. You know how impulsive I can be. Well, Pierre is the sensible one and has made me see that we have to work at a growing relationship. He was afraid I would have my fun with him, then leave and break his heart. He wouldn't let me do that. Don't you know, Uncle Lucas, how hard it is being away from the one you love?''

"Yes, Mimi. And I'm beginning to approve of this Pierre, but I'll reserve judgment until I see for myself." He unwrapped her arms and ignored her deflated look. "First, we have another matter that must be settled. It seems we have done this young lady a terrible injustice.''

Rae put her hand to her throat. What on earth did he mean? She looked at Andy, who had leaned forward, elbows on his knees, and was staring at the floor.

"You mean *me* ?" Rae gasped.

"Yes, I mean you," Lucas replied. "This entire summer has been a fiasco of lies, conniving, false pretenses, and taking advantage of you.''

"Nobody took advantage of me," she protested. "You've all been wonderful to me. I had nowhere else to go. Nothing to do.''

"Right," he said, his eyes bright.

Mimi meekly took a seat near Gran, who took her hand and patted it in a consoling gesture.

Lucas looked from one to the other. "You were supposed to be her friend, Mimi. Yet, knowing she had no one and had just lost her father, you did not offer her a home in the name of friendship, but as an accomplice to your brother's scheme."

He looked at Andy. "And Andy, you didn't offer this girl the job she needed as a gesture of kindness. You planned to use her for your own benefit."

Andy and Mimi paled under Lucas's stern gaze.

"What kind of friendship is that?" Lucas asked, staring at Mimi, who would not look at him.

"You wanted a real engagement, Andy. But how could she ever trust you to tell the truth? You think a girl wants to marry a man who has lied since the first moment she met him?"

"Please, Lucas," Rae began, but he silenced her with a look. "You'll have your turn. I'm talking to Mimi and Andy now."

Rae leaned back against the couch helplessly. Gran gave her a sympathetic look.

Mimi's lips trembled. "I'm sorry. It didn't seem so serious. It was just a little game to help Andy out of a spot. Rae needed a job, and I thought it would be terrific if she and Andy got together. I was thinking of what might result from a summer spent together."

She lifted moist eyes to him. "It did occur to me to ask her here. But I was only going to be here a week before leaving for Paris. I guess my mind was on my trip. . ."

"Even in the midst of her trouble, she didn't hesitate to invite you into her home, did she?"

"You make it sound so reprehensible," Rae protested, unable to keep quiet.

"It is," Lucas replied.

"And Andy, did you think of the possibility of Rae's falling in love with you? She had nothing and no one. You were offering her a world of plenty. Suppose she had fallen in love with you, but you couldn't return her love? Would you give her a car or jewelry, then tell her to run along?"

Andy was twisting his fingers uncomfortably as Lucas continued. "She wouldn't have accepted those things, Andy. She would have had nothing."

"You're right, Uncle Lucas," Andy agreed meekly. "I can't blame her for not loving me."

Rae fought the impulse to say she loved Andy, would marry him. Anything to stop this torture.

"All right," Lucas said. "So you two are sorry. And what do we do now? Mimi will go to Paris and marry her beloved Pierre. Andy will gallivant off to Switzerland and find someone else to console him while his heart is mending . . . But what about Ramona?"

Mimi rose and started toward Lucas. "You're not going to let me marry Pierre, are you? I know you won't! Oh, Uncle Lucas, I love him so. Don't you understand?" She was shaking her head, a fearful look in her eyes. Her voice became accusatory. "You don't know what it's like to love someone!"

"Oh, don't I, little girl?"

Mimi was properly chastened as he continued. "When love—what some people know as love— becomes the only important factor in a relationship, then it is a destructive element. Love can be a selfish thing, when all else is excluded. Real love is something that two must share, must build upon, must cherish. You might be able to survive it, to meet its challenge, if you give it the deference it deserves. But love can be as devastating as it is beautiful. And how do I know these things?" His tone was curt. "I've been around just a few years longer than you—and your uncle isn't immune to Cupid's fiery darts."

Mimi muttered a faint, "I'm sorry, Uncle Lucas."

Andy rose from the couch without looking at Lucas and walked over to the fireplace. He stood with his back to them. Rae saw that Gran's eyes were fastened on Lucas. When his eyes met hers, a smile settled about her lips. Lucas shifted uncomfortably and looked away from her.

When his gaze swept her way, Rae could not meet it. With bowed head she stared at the floor. Lucas had been, or was, in love. Perhaps he had discovered that Isobel was like that challenging mountain after all. Maybe that was part of the redeeming and devastating qualities about love; it wasn't particular about whom it attacked.

"Now sit down, Mimi," Lucas said sternly. She obeyed him, looking lost and forlorn. Rae's heart went out to her.

"What do you think I should do, Rae?" Lucas asked. "Is there any way we can make it up to you?"

Rae swallowed hard, not sure what to say. "Lucas, I know you feel you have to reprimand them because you're their guardian. But they didn't intend any harm. Intentions mean a lot. Mimi is my friend, and I've come to appreciate Andy. The job opportunity was a life-saver. Being here this summer has been—" she looked down at her hands clasped together "— the most wonderful time of my life in many ways. I don't blame Mimi and Andy. I'm grateful."

"Your opinion doesn't erase their guilt," he protested.

Mimi's sob was audible. She turned to Gran with pleading in her voice. "He's not going to let me marry Pierre."

"You're wrong, Mimi," Lucas said coldly. "If you want to go to Pierre right now, I'll write the check for your plane fare. You can have a new wardrobe. I'll finance the wedding. I'll hand over to you many times more than Rae has worked for all summer."

"And, Andy, I'm not going to disinherit you. You have money coming to you from your parents' estate. If you want to travel all over the world, I'll finance it, and deduct it from your inheritance. I'm not going to tell either of you what to do, so don't look so downcast. You're going to make your own decisions this time. Mimi, send your good friend a post card from Paris sometime. And, Andy, call her from Switzerland. Show her how much you care."

Andy turned and faced his uncle then. He looked crushed. "I would marry her if she'd have me, Uncle Lucas. That's how much I care. I'm not the insensitive cad you make me out to be. O.K. I was wrong. I admit that. But it's not the end of the world!"

"Isn't it?" Lucas asked abruptly. "I haven't finished."

CHAPTER 13

LUCAS LEANED FORWARD, his feet wide apart, his hands clasped between his knees. He stared at the floor for a moment, as if uncertain whether to speak. A weariness seemed to settle upon him. "You're right, Andy," he said slowly. "It's not the end of the world. Rather, it's the end of something that never really had a chance to begin."

He got up and walked around to the back of the couch, his fingers absently moving along the printed fabric. "I've given this a lot of thought. At first, I decided to remain silent, or perhaps talk to each of you separately. However," he drew in a deep breath, "since your offenses have been brought out and confessions made openly, I feel I should do the same."

"*You*, Uncle Lucas?" Mimi asked suddenly, disbelieving.

"I am the worst offender, Mimi," he assured. "I need to apologize and ask forgiveness, too. Just as you two of you have done." He looked from Rae, sitting by Gran, over to Andy by the fireplace.

He paced slowly as he talked, glancing occasionally at his audience "You see, from the first moment I saw Ramona, I wanted her for myself. My tactics were not exactly those befitting a gentleman. But I could not believe Andy had found a girl he really wanted to marry, and certainly not the kind I had always wanted for him. It seemed too sudden—too pat. I'll admit I was suspicious."

Lucas looked at Rae. She wondered what condemnation might follow now, but she was not prepared for the gentleness in his voice. "And Rae," he began, "when you and I sat on that mountain, with all of nature around us responding to the rising sun, something was happening inside myself. You needed me that morning. Like no woman ever has. It was like a revelation. You know, Andy," he said, turning his attention toward his nephew "the kind of girl I always said I wanted for you, was in reality the kind of woman I wanted for myself. It was wrong of me, I confess, but I sincerely hoped you were playing one of your games with me. And the only thing that prevented my telling Ramona was my belief that she might belong to *you* ."

Andy paled and could no longer look at his uncle.

"That morning, as the sun rose to warm our bodies, your inner beauty warmed my heart, Ramona," he said. "And if I hadn't been unsure of the relationship between you and Andy, I could have begun to love you then."

The sudden elation that had begun to soar in Rae plummeted to the depths. *Lucas could have loved me.*

163

But that was in the past. He said it was over, before it had a chance to begin.

She wanted to protest that it was not Andy who occupied her thoughts, who had stolen her heart, but she could not say such a thing in his presence. It was too late anyway.

Lucas asked that they bear with him just a little longer. Now that he had begun, he must say it all.

"Rae, when you asked me what kind of woman I wanted to marry, I couldn't be honest. But I want to be honest now. My fulfillment does not come in seeing the Grant label on sports equipment and clothing. Nor does it come from socializing at ski resorts. It comes from sharing myself with growing young men, who demand more of me that I normally would give. It comes from being a part of their spiritual and physical growth. It is my ministry in this life. I've always wanted a woman to share that ministry with me. But I could not say it, for I would have been telling Andy's woman that it was she who had captured my heart.

"You see, Andy," he said, turning to speak to his nephew who could not meet his eyes, "I would never betray you—even for the most marvelous woman I've ever met. So, I did the next best thing. I tried to arrange it so you two could have the life I wanted, working together in the two camps. And Rae," he said, his voice husky with emotion, "I'm so sorry that I was in a position that allowed you to witness my weaknesses, rather than my strength."

Rae felt the hot liquid scald her cheeks. She could hardly fathom his words. They were so beautiful, yet so terrible. So loving, yet so impossible. Each hope that rose in her was being dashed to pieces. There

164

were so many things she wanted to ask him, but this was not the place, not the time.

Then an uncontrollable sob escaped Mimi's throat. "Please, Uncle Lucas. We didn't mean to hurt you."

"I know that, Mimi. I'm not condemning you. I don't expect any of you to be perfect. We all know I'm not. But when we do wrong, we should be big enough to admit it, learn from it, and make it right if we can."

They each looked at him as if expecting answers. "I can't tell you what to do," he said. "You're adults now. You will have to find your own solutions."

Rae sat frozen in her seat, unable to lift a hand to wipe the tears from her face.

"Rae, I can understand if you have lost respect for this family. However, I know how much this summer meant to you. You are the kind of person who needs to give of herself, and those young people needed what you had to give. So, entirely separate from any family involvement, I'm offering you a job with the camp. You would work with Carl in the planning of the girls' camp, and if you would, direct it next summer. Otherwise I will have to abandon the project until a later date. But if you leave, as you have threatened to do, I wouldn't blame you. This family will never harbor any ill will toward you—whatever your decision."

Rae looked at him then, but before she could speak he said, "Now if you will all excuse me, I will be at Isobel's. There are some things I should have said to her a long time ago."

With that, he strode from the room, leaving them all in a state of shock. Gran dabbed at her eyes. Mimi sobbed aloud. Andy's face was pale.

Her heart sinking, Rae ran from the room. Just as she reached the deck, she heard his car retreating down the drive. She slumped, defeated, against the door frame.

Then Andy was standing beside her. "You love him, Rae?" She couldn't answer. "You do," he said incredulously. "You have all along. I can see it now."

"Oh, Andy, I'm sorry. I never intended to hurt you, or anyone else."

"I know," he said. "Nor did I. But I've done all sorts of damage with that impetuous scheme of mine. I can't blame you for loving Lucas, Rae. I'm not half the man he is. Maybe someday I'll deserve a girl like you."

"Andy, go after him. Tell him you don't love me."

"Rae," he said with determination, "I don't ever intend to lie to Uncle Lucas again. I'm sorry. I can't tell him that."

Andy turned and walked back through the house, leaving Rae staring out across the deck where she had first met Lucas. There had been a chance that he could love her. Now it was gone. And Lucas had turned to Isobel. If he made a commitment to her, he would never back away from it. He was that kind of man.

Rae didn't know where she would go, but she knew she could not be there when Lucas returned to announce his engagement to Isobel. He might even bring her back with him. . . . She was throwing things into her suitcases when Mimi came in.

"Oh, Rae," she wailed. "Do you hate me?"

"You know I don't, Mimi. Neither of you meant any real harm."

"Then why are you packing? Where are you going?"

Rae shrugged helplessly. "I don't know, but I can't stay here."

She tried to finish packing, but the blur before her eyes prevented her even seeing what she was doing. Collapsing on the bed, she let the tears come. Mimi was right beside her. "You love Lucas, Rae?"

"Doesn't everybody?" she asked miserably. "The girl on the diving board. Isobel. What difference does it make? He's gone, to Isobel."

"Let me help you pack," Mimi said, then added firmly. "We're going to Gran's."

"To Gran's?"

"Yes, we have a lot of thinking to do."

The following day Andy appeared on their doorstep, more exuberant than she had seen him in weeks. "I told Uncle Lucas! Rae," he said, taking her hands in his as they walked out back on the patio at Gran's house. "I told him about Switzerland. He liked the idea. I didn't think he would."

"That's wonderful, Andy. I know you'll make a success of that little shop."

"Go with me, Rae. We could have a good life together."

Rae was shaking her head. "You're a fine man, Andy. You'll find—"

"Don't say that," he interrupted. "It doesn't help. Maybe I've grown up a little. If I can't have you, then I hope you and Lucas get together, Rae. I really mean that."

She lowered her eyes. "It's much too late for that."

167

After a long moment, Andy leaned over and kissed her on the cheek.

"If you change your mind, let me know."

A week passed before Gran, Mimi, and Rae felt it was time to relate their plans to Lucas. The four of them sat in the padded redwood furniture on Gran's patio.

Tall frosted glasses of lemonade were a welcome respite from the warmth of August. After raising the back of the chaise, Mimi slipped out of her sandals, stretched her legs out and wiggled her red-painted toenails; Gran, nearby. Rae's and Lucas's glasses sat on a table between their chairs. Rae was grateful she didn't have to face Lucas, but could look out upon the dark green canopy of trees that obscured the view of nearby houses.

"I want to tell you what I've decided, Uncle Lucas," Mimi began hesitantly.

Lucas said nothing, waiting.

"I've decided to finish my senior year at the University in Asheville before marrying Pierre. I'm going to move in with Gran while going to school. It will be easier since Rae refuses to move to the Haven, and I need her to help me with wedding plans."

Rae suddenly realized Lucas might want Isobel to help with the wedding. That would be logical if he were planning his own marriage. "You may have other plans, Lucas. This is a big event and I'm sure there's more expert advice available than mine."

"We'll hire all the experts we need," Lucas assured her. "But I'm not making Mimi's decisions any longer. And I can readily understand her wanting a friend to talk things over with."

168

"I want you to be proud of me, Uncle Lucas," Mimi said, as if being released from his dominion was not as appealing as it might once have seemed.

"Your decision to finish school before getting married could not have been an easy one, Mimi, but I feel it is a wise one. There are many plans to be made in Paris. To show you how proud I am of you, I'm sending the three of you to Paris during Christmas holidays."

Before Rae could protest, Mimi shrieked, jumped up, ran over to her uncle, and hugged him fiercely. "Oh, I love you, Uncle Lucas!" and in the next breath added, "I've got to go call Pierre and tell him."

"Then you're not going to Paris, Lucas?" Gran asked.

"No, at least not now." he replied. "I plan to fly to Switzerland and spend Christmas with Andy."

Gran looked at Mimi's sandals, left behind in her haste to call Pierre. "I'd better go remind that girl whose telephone she's using for that Paris call." She went inside the house.

Rae reached for her glass, thinking she might join the women, but Lucas spoke. "Carl tells me you're on the permanent payroll as of Monday."

Rae leaned back, looking out where the sun was retreating. "I have no real ties in Atlanta," she said, beginning to relate her decisions, a result of much thinking and praying during the past week. "The job you offered me is a place where I can share with others the faith and values my father stood for, and have become a part of my own sense of purpose and commitment. If you agree, I'll work with Carl, then help direct the girls camp next summer. You have a wonderful ministry, and I'm honored that you want me to be a part of it."

He stood and stepped over in front of her, looking down. "Without you, those dreams of mine could not materialize for next summer." She must have been mistaken in thinking his hands moved forward as if to reach for her, and that his eyes held a kind of excitement, for he straightened, silhouetted against slopes darkened by a dying sun.

"Any ideas you have will be welcomed, Rae. After you have worked with Carl for a while, we'll discuss the plans and decide exactly what direction to take. And believe me when I say we are fortunate to have you join our staff."

They didn't see Lucas for a while. Gran said he was committed to several meetings and speaking engagements. A former gold-medal winner was always in demand.

Rae shared her letters from Andy with Mimi and Gran. He was now co-owner of the little shop and apparently loved every minute of it. He said he might go big-time and expand, possibly handling Lucas's sports equipment and clothing and opening a branch office.

"There isn't much time for girls, Rae," he wrote. "But I manage to see them occasionally. I hope you get all the good things you deserve. Give my love to Uncle Lucas."

I wish I could give him mine, she thought, putting down the letter.

Since Lucas was away on business most of the time, he made the house and lake available to Gran, Mimi and Rae during fall break.

Even when Lucas was in the house, Rae never found herself alone with him. It was as if he were deliberately avoiding her. He seemed to want her to understand that the awakening love he had thought possible had fled. It would never surface again.

The day before he was to leave for the North Carolina resort, then Switzerland, dawned bright and clear. He drove the Lincoln up the Parkway with Gran in front; Mimi and Rae, in back.

"Of all the seasons in the mountains, I do believe fall is the most beautiful," Rae exclaimed when they stopped at Craggy Gardens. "I've never seen such spectacular colors." The mountainsides were splashed with brilliant reds, golds, oranges, greens, yellows, deep, rich colors that gleamed in the sunlight.

Lucas moved close, pointing out the garden before them. "Magnificent," he said, then their eyes met. "You'll never want to leave the mountains, will you?"

"No," she said. She would like to come to this spot again, remembering the man who might have loved her. What might have been. What was no more.

They walked back to the car, and Lucas drove higher and higher, where the balsams were scarce, their limbs growing on only one side of the trunks. Many trees were bent, all in the same direction. Others were lying on rocky ground.

"The winds," Lucas explained, "are terrific up here in the wintertime. These roads are closed and there's snow on Mt. Mitchell most of the season."

Fog, mist, and clouds obscured much of the view from the lookout. *Does Lucas remember holding me in the early morning mist?* Rae wondered.

Lucas was to leave right after breakfast the next morning. Rae didn't sleep well, thinking about it.

When breakfast was served, she ran down the stairs, calling over her shoulder, "I'll eat later." She didn't want Mimi to have a chance to ask where she was going, or offer to go with her.

Running down the mountain to the lakeshore, she shed her shorts, shirt, tennis shoes, and the towel she had around her neck. Clad in a bathing suit, she ran around to the deeper part of the lake, jumped in, swam back to the shallow side, then climbed out and lay on her back on the towel, allowing the early morning sunshine to dry her.

It was quite cool at first, but soon the constant rays of the October sun warmed her skin, causing her to doze off. She must have slept about thirty minutes before she was awakened by the sound of a car coming down the gravel road. She didn't want to say good-by. She didn't move, not even when she heard the footsteps on the wooden planks.

CHAPTER 14

SITTING UP, SHE reached for her shirt and slipped her arms through the sleeves.

"I'm a mess," she said.

"You're always saying that," Lucas replied, reaching out to touch her tangled curls. "Crazy, the way your hair curls like that."

Her heart skipped a beat, and when he spoke again, it was about trivialities.

"You haven't seen the place in wintertime," he said and she shook her head. "You'll love it when it snows. Light a fire in the fireplace in the lounge."

She looked up at him and he was staring at the mountainsides on the other side of the lake. "All right, Lucas. Thank you."

"Any message for Andy?"

"Tell him I hope he's well." Lucas looked at her sharply. "I didn't mean to hurt him, Lucas."

"I know that, Rae. It's just hard for me to grasp sometimes that you really aren't Andy's girl. And never were." His voice was distant and saddened. "Do you think he will ever stop loving you?"

"Of course," she replied quickly.

Lucas sighed. "It can be pretty miserable, pining away for a girl who can't be yours. But I suppose the way to know for sure is to ask him. I'll be back." he assured with a smile, then walked toward his car. got in, and waved as he drove away.

Rae lifted her hand, but did not smile, as the black Lincoln moved away from her, down the gravel road.

The leaves lost their brilliance and fell to the ground, reflecting the bleakness of Rae's world without Lucas. But the prospect of Paris was exciting, and Mimi's exuberance proved contagious.

The trip was far from a sightseeing tour, however. Christmas Day was spent with many guests, including Pierre's family, at the Doudets' fashionable Parisian home. Most of the conversation centered around the wedding. It seemed all of Paris held or attended a party for Mimi.

The highlight of the season was a card from Lucas which read: "How do you like Paris? The snow here is great. See you in a few weeks. Lucas."

Back in North Carolina ice and sleet marked January and February. Mimi's classes were cancelled several times and Rae didn't even attempt to drive to the campgrounds.

Then the rains came, accompanied by swollen streams and flood watches. Mimi laughingly called it "liquid sunshine" and marked the days off on the calendar.

Finally the warm rays of sunshine began to dry the saturated earth and tiny green shoots made their appearance. Lucas appeared, too, in early spring, during Mimi's break from school. He and Carl finalized camp plans to allow Rae time to help plan Mimi's farewell party at The Haven. She wouldn't be seeing her friends for a while after leaving for Paris.

The April showers ceased long enough for the sun to shine on the day of the party. A fabulous dinner was followed by a surprise "This Is Your Life" game in which some of Mimi's childhood escapades were revealed.

"Tell us about the wedding," was all Mimi needed to fill the next hour with details. "All of you are invited," she said at last. "It's a huge wedding. Since Pierre teaches at the university, all the faculty and administration are invited, along with students. *Grandmere* and *Grandpere* know everyone in Paris, as do Pierre's family. Uncle Lucas has friends and business acquaintances there, not to mention my own friends."

Lucas held up a restraining hand. "Why don't you just invite the whole world?" he boomed.

Mimi looked surprised. "I thought we had!" She laughed and went over to hug him.

"At least it's only once," he said affectionately. "How long until you graduate?"

"Seven weeks," she replied. "Then I'll have my degree. I'm on a rain break right now."

"Why don't you all stay here tonight?" Lucas suggested after Mimi's friends had gone.

"I don't have to be asked twice," Gran replied, walking out of the lounge toward the stairway. "Good night."

"What does one do with five toasters?" Mimi

asked, then cut her eyes around at Lucas. "I'll bet you think I don't know what to do with one."

"Do you?"

"No," she admitted, and grinned. "But I do know I have to write some thank–you notes." With that, she began to rummage around in boxes scattered all over the lounge floor until she found the note papers. Then, with a cheery wave of her hand, she hurried up the stairs.

"Let's have a cup of coffee," Lucas suggested to Rae when the excitement had died down.

Selma was leaving the kitchen when they walked in. "There's fresh coffee in the pot," she said and shook her head, a knowing smile on her lips. Someone *would* start dirtying dishes after she had just cleaned the kitchen.

Lucas took two cups from the cupboard and poured while Rae sat at the table. "I'm bushed," she admitted, rubbing the back of her neck.

"I can imagine," Lucas symphathized, bringing the coffee over. "My main role is bill-payer, and I'm ready to call it quits for at least another twenty years or so."

Yes, Rae thought, *if he marries Isobel, and has children of his own, he probably will be ready to give away a daughter at the altar at just about that time.*

Refusing to entertain such a dismal thought, Rae mentioned the project that was uppermost in both their minds. "It's amazing how much progress has been made on the new camp," she said. "The gym is ready, the cabins built, and Carl says the pool will be finished within a month after the rains stop and the crews can resume work."

"And in two short months, your young girls will be here," he added.

Rae glanced over at him and smiled. "I remember your telling me that about the boys' camp. I couldn't have dreamed of the excitement and wonder of being involved in their lives. Oh, Lucas, it's so exciting to see the applications coming in, reading about those fresh-faced young girls with their goals and ambitions. It's such a tremendous challenge that I sometimes wonder if I can possibly live up to the responsibility."

"I have confidence in you, Rae. I brought some folders up that I want to look over with you. That is, if you're not too tired."

"Oh, not at all." Rae drained her cup, wondering if she had reacted too enthusiastically. "Talking about something other than the wedding is refreshing."

Lucas pushed his chair away from the table. "I'll meet you in the study in a little while."

Rae went to the room she had occupied when she had first come to the Haven. She turned in front of the mirror, as if expecting something to be out of place. It wasn't. Not even her hair, for it still fell softly along one side of her face and was brushed back on the other, exposing a small gold earring, matching her choker.

The soft green knit dress was the color of early spring leaves and suitable for this in-between weather. She applied a bronzed gloss to her lips and noticed the unnatural brightness of her eyes, and the flush on her cheeks. *How ridiculous,* she told herself, *to have a rapid heartbeat over a business meeting with an employer*.

Lucas was already in the study when Rae arrived. He had removed his suit coat and tie, and his sleeves were rolled up as if he were ready to work. "I thought we'd be more comfortable on the couch than sitting at the desk," he said.

Rae sat on the couch near him. Folders were spread out on the coffee table. He began to discuss the staff and soon Rae was recommending counselors, activity directors, skills leaders, and even talked about interviewing secretaries to work only for the girls camp.

"Much of the decision making is up to you, Rae," Lucas reminded her.

"I appreciate your confidence in me," she said gratefully. "But I'm not as experienced as you are."

"Your sensitivity to the inner needs of the girls is important," he assured. "It would be easy to overlook that and focus on what we offer in the way of physical facilities and equipment. Your suggestion of having Marge serve as sort of mother figure is an excellent one. Each of us needs someone to share our feelings with, don't we?"

Rae nodded, not daring to look at him.

"You can't imagine what this means to me, Rae, the two of us working together like this. I've always dreamed of . . ."

His words were interrupted by a light tapping on the door. Mimi walked in. "I'm going to bed. Night has long passed, so I'll say good morning." She handed them each a piece of paper, then walked away, yawning.

"Oh, Lucas, look. Thank-you notes."

He smiled down at the loving words Mimi had written. "I've trained her well."

"You've met Pierre now, haven't you? Do you approve?"

"I think so. He's a very dashing fellow. Not the

178

stereotyped teacher at all. He's tall, good-looking, a sports enthusiast. And Mimi is impressed with his mind—and his heart. He counsels many of his students, I understand." He turned a little to face Rae. "And he's several years older than Mimi. She needs someone like that, I believe. All those years I felt they needed me," Lucas smiled reflectively, "I needed them just as much."

"We all need people," she said and realized she mustn't stare into his wonderful face so intently. Suddenly she had to know. "Are you going to marry Isobel?"

Surprise flooded his face. "Never!" he responded immediately. "What gave you that idea?"

"Well, you said you had to get things settled. I assumed . . ."

"I meant I had to be honest with her and let her know there's not a chance of that. I never said there was."

Mimi's thank-you note was becoming wrinkled from the pressure of her fingers, so she reached over and laid it on the coffee table. His sudden question surprised her.

"Do you not love Andy a little?"

"Yes," she answered honestly. "I love Andy a lot. Like I do Mimi. I want to see them happy."

"Was there some glaring reason why you couldn't marry him?"

"Yes, Lucas. I'm not in love with Andy." Her finger nervously traced a pattern on the knit dress.

"I think his broken heart is healing," Lucas assured. "Otherwise I don't think he would even look at another girl."

"I'm glad," she said sincerely.

179

His hand reached out and covered hers. "I've waited a long time for that, Rae. I could not approach you as long as I felt Andy was in love with you, or there was a chance for the two of you. Even though you can't love me, Rae, perhaps you and I . . . ."

"What. . . .what do you mean . . . if I can't love you?" she asked haltingly, her green eyes full of wonder.

"Well," Lucas said hesitantly. "It was pretty clear. When I admitted my love for you, you said nothing."

"When was that?" she asked, amazed.

"The night I admitted to the family how I felt about you from the moment I saw you," he said with incredulity.

"But Lucas, you talked as if that was something in the past. That you *might* have loved me, but that it never had a chance."

He was shaking his head. "Rae, I thought you would know what I meant. I couldn't be so blunt in front of Andy. He was still hurting. I tried to make myself clear, so that you would understand."

"Lucas," she said, glad recognition dawning in her eyes. "A person doesn't *assume* a thing like that. It has to be said. And the night I tried to tell you how I felt, you stopped me."

"You mean, when you said you cared?"

She nodded.

"I thought you were going to tell me that you belonged to Andy. I stopped you because I couldn't stand to hear it. Ramona," he said suddenly, "could we start over?"

"No, Lucas," she said. "I can only *continue*. I began to love you long ago. I love you still—now and always."

"Just so there is no further misunderstanding, let me say, I love you, too. And I want to marry you right away."

"Oh, Lucas!" she cried, her heart overflowing with love for him. "But when will I ever find time now. The camp—the girls—"

"You'll *make* time." His laughter exploded from deep within. "Even if I have to fire you! And I'm not waiting twenty years. But I suppose you want a big wedding like Mimi."

Rae shook her head.

"A small one. Maybe in Gran's church. I do want to walk down the aisle in white, toward my husband-to-be. Maybe Marge as matron of honor and Mimi as bridesmaid. Nothing elaborate, just simple and beautiful. Then a small reception with a few of your friends and those I've come to know from camp."

"That sounds perfect," Lucas said in amazement. "How long have you had this planned?"

"Well," she said, a lovely glow on her face, "I've never thought of the wedding before, but I have dreamed of spending my life with you. That's the important part."

"We should be married before we go to Paris for Mimi's wedding," Lucas said. "We can have a short honeymoon there before coming back for the camping season. We won't have much time together for a while."

"We'll have a lifetime."

"Yes," he sighed, "a lifetime."

"Lucas," she said quietly. "Why don't you stop looking at me, and take me in your arms. That's where I belong. Where I want to be."

"I've spent almost a year trying not to do that. I'm

afraid I will take you in my arms only to awaken and find this is all a dream. Just like that first morning. It was a nightmare, Ramona, thinking you could never be mine."

"I know, Lucas. I felt that way, too."

Still holding her hand, he stood and gently pulled her to her feet. "Come on," he said, and led her through the house and out onto the deck and down to the third one, where they had met that first morning.

They stood looking out upon the dark green foliage and upward toward the smoky gray haze lingering along the peaks, visible evidence that the moisture had risen from the forest floor.

"This setting will always be a reminder to me, Lucas," Rae said regretfully, "of all the misunderstandings and heartaches of the past year."

"Yes, Ramona, but beyond that darkness is the beginning of a new day."

One arm went around her shoulder and he held her close as he pointed with the other hand. "Look. You can see it. There in the gap between those highest peaks."

Rae could see the faint fingers of dawn just beginning to reach into the shadowed coves and hollows.

"It's like us, Lucas," Rae whispered. "Like all human beings. "The sun doesn't move—it's the earth that turns away, causing the night. God doesn't move—we look away from Him, bringing darkness into our own lives."

Lucas was nodding his agreement. "And like our love. It didn't disappear. It was there, waiting for us until we could recognize it and express it in the right way, and at the right time."

As they watched, the glow spread along the ridges, dispelling the last shadows, touching the smoky haze and turning it to gold.

Lucas drew Rae closer into his arms. His dark eyes mirrored the majesty of the awakening mountains. "Ramona, I love you."

She lifted her face for the touch of his lips on hers. Neither of them turned to watch the sun rise higher into the vaulted sky, feeling only the warmth of its gentle caress.

ABOUT THE AUTHOR

YVONNE LEHMAN is an award-winning novelist and founder of the Blue Ridge Christian Writers Conference held annually at Blue Ridge Assembly, Black Mountain, North Carolina, which serves as the enchanting setting for this, her fifth published novel. She is listed in *Who's Who of America*, *Personalities of the South*, *Contemporary Authors*, and *International Authors & Writers Who's Who* among others.

Yvonne is also a wife and mother of four, and resides with her family in Black Mountain.

A Letter To Our Readers

Dear Reader:

Pioneering is an exhilarating experience, filled with opportunities for exploring new frontiers. The Zondervan Corporation is proud to be the first major publisher to launch a series of inspirational romances designed to inspire and uplift as well as to provide wholesome entertainment. In order that we might better contribute to your reading enjoyment, we would appreciate your taking a few minutes to respond to the following questions and return to:

Anne Severance, Editor
Serenade/Saga Books
749 Templeton Drive
Nashville, Tennessee   37205

1. Did you enjoy reading SMOKY MOUNTAIN SUN-RISE?

☐ Very much. I would like to see more books by this author!
☐ Moderately
☐ I would have enjoyed it more if _____

2. Where did you purchase this book? _____

3. What influenced your decision to purchase this book?
☐ Cover   ☐ Back cover copy
☐ Title   ☐ Friends
☐ Publicity   ☐ Other _____

4. Please rate the following elements from 1 (poor) to 10 (superior):

☐ Heroine   ☐ Plot
☐ Hero   ☐ Inspirational theme
☐ Setting   ☐ Secondary characters

5. Which settings would you like to see in future Serenade/Saga Books?

_____   _____

_____   _____

6. What are some inspirational themes you would like to see treated in Serenade books?

_____   _____

_____   _____

7. Would you be interested in reading other Serenade/Serenata or Serenade/Saga Books?

☐ Very interested
☐ Moderately interested
☐ Not interested

8. Please indicate your age range:

☐ Under 18   ☐ 25–34   ☐ 46–55
☐ 18–24   ☐ 35–45   ☐ Over 55

9. Would you be interested in a Serenade book club? If so, please give us your name and address:

Name _____

Occupation _____

Address _____

City _____ State _____ Zip _____

Serenade/Serenata Books are inspirational romances in contemporary settings, designed to bring you a joyful, heart-lifting reading experience.

Other Serenade books available in your local bookstore:

#1 ON WINGS OF LOVE, Elaine L. Schulte
#2 LOVE'S SWEET PROMISE,
     Susan C. Feldhake
#3 FOR LOVE ALONE, Susan C. Feldhake
#4 LOVE'S LATE SPRING, Lydia Heermann
#5 IN COMES LOVE, Mab Graff Hoover
#6 FOUNTAIN OF LOVE, Velma S. Daniels and
     Peggy E. King.
#7 MORNING SONG, Linda Herring
#8 A MOUNTAIN TO STAND STRONG, Peggy
     Darty
#9 LOVE'S PERFECT IMAGE, Judy Baer

Coming in the months ahead:

OCT. *Serenade/Saga*
#10 LOVE BEYOND SURRENDER, Susan C.
     Feldhake

NOV. *Serenade/Serenata*
#11 GREENGOLD AUTUMN, Donna Fletcher
     Crow

DEC. *Serenade/Saga*
#11 ALL THE DAYS AFTER SUNDAY, Jeanette
     Gilge

Serenade/Saga Books are historical inspirational romances, and are available wherever Serenade Books are sold.